You're About to Become a

Privileged *Woman*.

INTRODUCING
PAGES & PRIVILEGES™.

It's our way of thanking you for buying
our books at your favorite retail store.

GET ALL THIS *FREE*
WITH JUST ONE PROOF OF PURCHASE:

◆ **Hotel Discounts** up
to 60% at home and
abroad ◆ **Travel Service**
- Guaranteed lowest
published airfares
plus 5% cash back
on tickets ◆ **$25 Travel Voucher**

$50 VALUE

◆ **Sensuous Petite Parfumerie** collection

◆ **Insider Tips Letter**
with sneak previews
of upcoming books

You'll get a FREE personal card, too.
It's your passport to all these benefits— and to
even more great gifts & benefits to come!

There's no club to join. No purchase commitment. No obligation.

Enrollment Form

☐ *Yes!* I WANT TO BE A *Privileged Woman*.

Enclosed is one *PAGES & PRIVILEGES*™ Proof of Purchase from any Harlequin or Silhouette book currently for sale in stores (Proofs of Purchase are found on the back pages of books) and the store cash register receipt. Please enroll me in *PAGES & PRIVILEGES*™. Send my Welcome Kit and FREE Gifts -- and activate my FREE benefits -- immediately.

More great gifts and benefits to come like these luxurious Truly Lace and L'Effleur gift baskets.

▶ ▶ DETACH HERE AND MAIL TODAY! ▶

NAME (please print)
_____

ADDRESS _____ APT. NO _____

CITY _____ STATE _____ ZIP/POSTAL CODE _____

| PROOF OF PURCHASE | **NO CLUB!** |
| SAMPLE ONLY | **NO COMMITMENT!** |

**NO CLUB!
NO COMMITMENT!**
*Just one purchase brings you great **Free Gifts** and **Benefits!***
(More details in back of this book.)

Please allow 6-8 weeks for delivery. Quantities are limited. We reserve the right to substitute items. Enroll before October 31, 1995 and receive one full year of benefits.

Name of store where this book was purchased_____

Date of purchase_____

Type of store:

☐ Bookstore   ☐ Supermarket   ☐ Drugstore

☐ Dept. or discount store (e.g. K-Mart or Walmart)

☐ Other (specify)_____

Which Harlequin or Silhouette series do you usually read?

Complete and mail with one Proof of Purchase and store receipt to:

U.S.: *PAGES & PRIVILEGES*™, P.O. Box 1960, Danbury, CT 06813-1960

Canada: *PAGES & PRIVILEGES*™, 49-6A The Donway West, P.O. 813, North York, ON M3C 2E8   **PRINTED IN U.S.A**

"You Feel Guilty Because Every Time You Look At Me You See Your Brother's Face,"

Annie said heavily. "But you know why I feel guilty, Jared?"

Her voice was so quiet he could barely hear her.

"Because every time you look at me," she said, her words shaking, "every time you touch me, I can't even remember what Jonathan looked like."

She turned and walked away. He wanted to call out to her, to jump out of the truck and bring her back to him. To hold her in his arms and tell her that it was all right.

But it wasn't all right. And it never would be.

So he watched her go.

Dear Reader,

Imagine that you're single, and you've been longing for a family all your life…but there aren't any husband prospects in sight. Then suddenly, a handsome, sexy rancher offers you a proposition: marry him. The catch—you've got to help raise his four rambunctious children. It's tempting…but is it practical? That's the dilemma faced by Kara Kirby in this month's MAN OF THE MONTH, *The Wilde Bunch* by Barbara Boswell. What does Kara do? I'm not telling—you have to read the book!

And a new miniseries begins, MEN OF THE BLACK WATCH, with *Heart of the Hunter* by BJ James. The "Black Watch" is a top-secret organization whose agents face danger every day, but now face danger of a different sort—the danger of losing your heart when you fall in love.

In addition, the CODE OF THE WEST series continues with Luke's story in *Cowboys Don't Quit* by Anne McAllister. And the HEART OF STONE series continues with *Texas Temptation* by Barbara McCauley.

For a light, romantic romp don't miss Karen Leabo's *Man Overboard;* and a single dad gets saddled with a batch of babies in *The Rancher and the Redhead* by Suzannah Davis.

I hope you enjoy them all—I certainly do!

Lucia Macro
Senior Editor

Please address questions and book requests to:
Silhouette Reader Service
U.S.: 3010 Walden Ave., P.O. Box 1325, Buffalo, NY 14269
Canadian: P.O. Box 609, Fort Erie, Ont. L2A 5X3

BARBARA McCAULEY
TEXAS TEMPTATION

SILHOUETTE *Desire*®
Published by Silhouette Books
America's Publisher of Contemporary Romance

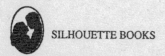

SILHOUETTE BOOKS

ISBN 0-373-05948-5

TEXAS TEMPTATION

Copyright © 1995 by Barbara Joel

Books by Barbara McCauley

Silhouette Desire

Woman Tamer #621
Man From Cougar Pass #698
Her Kind of Man #771
Whitehorn's Woman #803
A Man Like Cade #832
Nightfire #875
*Texas Heat #917
*Texas Temptation #948

*Hearts of Stone

BARBARA McCAULEY

was born and raised in California and has spent a good
portion of her life exploring the mountains, beaches
and deserts so abundant there. The youngest of five
children, she grew up in a small house, and her only
chance for a moment alone was to sneak into the back-
yard with a book and quietly hide away.

With two children of her own now and a busy house-
hold, she still finds herself slipping away to enjoy a
good novel. A daydreamer and incurable romantic, she
says writing has fulfilled her most incredible dream of
all—breathing life into the people in her mind and
making them real. She has two loud and demanding
Amazon parrots named Fred and Barney, and when
she can manage the time, she loves to sink her hands
into fresh-turned soil and make things grow.

To Liz Cutler,
a good friend and fellow writer whose knowledge is
impressive and patience immeasurable.

One

A storm was coming.

It moved in swiftly from the south, thick swelling clouds carried in by a hot heavy wind that swept the harsh West Texas land. Lightning split the dark horizon, illuminating the distant mountains. The air trembled in anticipation of the coming rain.

Jared Stone sat on the steps of the trailer he'd called home for the past eight months and watched the electrical display zigzag across the night sky. Jagged fingers of brilliant silver light flashed repeatedly, but there was no thunder. Not yet, anyway. Just the deafening echo of silence.

Lifting the bottle to his mouth, Jared tossed back a long swallow of rotgut whiskey, then grimaced as the liquid burned his throat and settled in his stomach with a kick strong enough to send a football two hundred yards.

Strange, but he'd actually come to enjoy that part.

The wind slid over Jared's bare chest like sun-warmed silk, and the sensation made him think of a woman's hands. Frowning, he stared into the darkness, wondering if he'd deprived himself of feminine company for so long as punishment or simply because he hadn't had the time.

Jared stared at the bottle in his hand. "What do you think?" he asked his companion.

Thunder rumbled in the distance. He glanced up at the sound and stared out into the darkness, but there was nothing to see. Nothing but the silhouette of a one-hundred-foot oil derrick staring back at him from almost a half mile away. A flash of lightning illuminated the tower, and Jared's hand tightened around the bottle. It was impossible to stop the image that flashed in his mind for what seemed like the thousandth time....

Jonathan.

Jared squeezed his eyes shut and drew in a sharp breath. Almost four years had not dulled the memory of his twin brother's death. There'd been a storm that night, too. No one should have been up on the rig. Especially Jonathan. He'd been too green, too inexperienced. And at twenty-nine, too damn young.

Since they'd been ten years old, both Jonathan and Jared had dreamed of building their own oil well, despite the fact they came from a family of ranchers. It had taken ten years after graduating high school to convince their father, J.T., to back the project, but they'd finally worn him down. Jonathan, who'd returned to college in his late twenties to get his master's degree in geology, and Jared, with ten years' experience working every rig that would hire him, were ready to start drilling. They'd both believed in the well; both been equally determined to hit oil.

But one had died.

In his grief, J. T. Stone had closed the rig down after Jonathan's accident, despite Jared's argument that doing so meant that Jonathan would have died for nothing. But J.T. had insisted, and the project was abandoned, leaving the derrick and equipment to the elements of a lonely West Texas plain called Stone Creek.

Until now.

Jared took another pull of the whiskey. If only he hadn't left in anger for South America right after his brother's funeral and not come back. If only his father hadn't died so unexpectedly eight months ago. If only...

Damn you, Jonathan Stone.

Jared threw the bottle, and lightning flashed as the sound of shattering glass rent the air. Clouds were moving in quickly now; the wind whipped at the ends of Jared's dark hair. He stared at the derrick, cursing the wooden beast as if it were a living thing.

Since he'd come back, everyone had told him to give up. Sell the land or lease it out. There'd been no oil drilling on Stone Creek for three years. It was ranch land. His stepmother, Myrna, pestered him continually to sell his fifteen thousand acres, but Jared had flatly refused. His great-great-grandfather had bought this land with a lick and a promise, and that was all Jared had now, too.

Only Jake, his older brother, and Jessica, his younger sister, never questioned or discouraged him. Each of them had their own legacy of Stone Creek: Jake, sixty thousand acres of ranch, and Jessica, fifteen thousand acres, which included the abandoned town of Makeshift. Each of them understood they needed to safeguard their inheritance their own way.

Even his nine-year-old half sister, Emma, had painted a picture of a gushing oil well and told him to put it on his refrigerator where he could see it every day.

If only the investors would be so optimistic.

Jared had already mortgaged the land and used every penny of the money J.T. had left him to start drilling again. But it wasn't enough. He needed a backer, and the only company that hadn't turned him down yet was a Dallas-based company, Arloco Oil.

Arloco was Jared's last hope. Without their backing, he'd have to shut down. Something had to happen. And it had to happen soon.

Another bolt of lightning struck, close by this time. Rain bounced off the dry earth, scattered at first, then building in speed and intensity as the storm settled in.

Jared lifted his face to the sky and welcomed the feel of the rain on his skin. The sky lit up again and the ground shook from the accompanying thunder.

She was miles away and yet she could see it.

It loomed in the distance, growing larger and taller with every passing mile. Her heart pounded at the sight. It was as beautiful as it was foreboding. As promising as it was hopeless. As seductive as it was frightening.

Excitement coursed through her as she drew closer. She'd been twenty-three the summer Jonathan had brought her home with him to introduce her to his family and show her the rig. She'd never forget the pride in his eyes when he'd showed her the derrick. Every foot of that well had been a labor of love for Jonathan and his brother Jared.

The odds against actually finding oil were horrendous; roughly ninety percent of the wells never hit. But neither Jonathan nor Jared had even considered that possibility. She'd had the feeling they would have drilled to the center of the earth and headed for China before they gave up. She smiled at the thought. No, that probably still wouldn't have discouraged them. They hadn't been identical in looks, but they'd certainly been identical in determination.

And now Jared was back.

Annie's palms were sweaty as she pulled in front of the trailer where Jonathan had brought her four years ago. The same trailer where he'd proposed. The same trailer where he'd made love to her for the first time.

And for the last time.

She'd left Jonathan there that summer and gone home to finish her last year of school. How could she have known she'd never see him again?

Her hand shook as she opened the driver's door of her Cherokee, and when she stepped out the ground felt unsteady under her boot. The clouds had moved on from the storm last night, leaving a deep blue sky and the scent of fresh damp earth. She'd loved Stone Creek the minute she'd laid eyes on the open land. She and Jonathan had been going to build a house not far from here; they'd even marked off the spot with rocks and pieces of wood.

She didn't know where that spot was anymore.

Annie turned and stared at the derrick, letting her gaze slowly scan the length of it from bottom to top. She remembered the day Jonathan had scaled the rigging, teasing her until she came up and joined him. She'd been terrified as she'd climbed, but he'd sweet-talked her the whole way, telling her he'd never let any harm come to her....

If only she could have done the same for him.

Her eyes started to blur and she blinked rapidly, swallowing the lump in her throat.

Nights had been the hardest after Jonathan's death. One day had become another, until a year had finally passed, then another and another. She'd stayed busy with school, then work. And slowly, without her even realizing it, the darkness began to lift.

She still missed him, she always would, but she'd finally managed to say goodbye.

She stared at the trailer again and hesitated, suddenly overcome with a desire to get back in her car and leave. Jared wouldn't want to see her, she was sure of that. There were enough painful memories of Jonathan around here. She knew how hard Jared had taken Jonathan's death, and she would be one more reminder to him that his brother was dead.

Heart hammering, she moved toward the trailer, then drew in a deep breath and knocked on the door.

Nothing.

She knocked again. Louder.

Still nothing.

Frowning, Annie stared at the door. It was only ten o'clock. She could see there was no activity at the rig, so she doubted he was there. She started to turn away, thinking he might have gone into town, but there was a dusty black pickup parked in front of the trailer. He should be here. He was supposed to—

The sound of breaking glass from inside the trailer cut her thoughts short. She drew her brows together, then turned the knob and opened the door.

It was dark inside. The scent of cold coffee and wet clothes filled the trailer, and she nearly stumbled over a pair of damp jeans lying by the front door.

"Jared?" she called hesitantly. An unintelligible response came from the bedroom.

She took a shaky step toward the sound, then stopped. Dear Lord, what if he had someone with him and she was intruding? She started to turn away, but another cry came from the bedroom, one filled with such anguish that she couldn't possibly ignore it.

Heart pounding, she moved through the living area, stepping around a large map laid out on the tiled floor. Smaller maps covered a brown fabric couch, and several bottles containing soil samples were lined up on an oval pine coffee table.

The bedroom door was ajar, and her fingers were trembling as she placed her hand on the knob and pushed. The room was in near darkness, except for the glow of a clock on the nightstand. A half-empty bottle of whiskey sat beside the clock.

"Jared?" She stepped closer to the bed.

At least he was alone, she noted. He moved restlessly in his sleep, tossing the covers off his shoulders and uttering another low moan.

Was he sick?

She couldn't see his face because he was lying on his stomach, facedown in his pillow, his fists clenched tightly beside his head. Her heart thundered in her chest as she reached out a shaky hand to touch his bare shoulder. He mumbled something incoherent and his muscle twitched at her touch. His skin was hot and damp with sweat.

She leaned over the bed. "Jared, are you all—"

He moved so fast she hadn't time to react. His hand snaked out and grabbed her wrist, pulling her into the bed with him as he kicked the covers off completely. In less than a heartbeat he had her underneath him and his long hard body stretched out over her.

His *naked* body.

She sucked in a sharp breath, and in the next moment his lips closed over hers. She opened her mouth to say something, but his tongue invaded, kissing her with more passion, more desperation, than she could have dreamed possible.

Panic consumed her. Her cry was muffled against his mouth, and when she placed her palms against his chest and pushed she might as well have tried to bench press a two-hundred-pound weight.

Annie's mind raced. Her heart pounded. *Stay calm,* she told herself. He was obviously still asleep, or else he thought she was someone else. As soon as she could manage to say something, he'd realize what he was doing and stop. There was no need for her to worry. Jared would never hurt her, she was sure of that.

At least, she *thought* she was sure.

His lips moved over hers in a rhythm as timeless as it was sensual, and she felt herself go weak with the force of his kiss. He moaned again, and this time there was no doubt it was pleasure, not illness or pain. The need she heard and felt from him vibrated through her, sending shivers of electricity coursing through her body.

It had been so long since a man had kissed her like this, like he wanted to consume her, and longer still since she'd felt even a spark of response. He deepened the kiss, slanting his mouth hard against her own, taking her again and again with a wild abandon that left her breathless.

And undeniably excited.

This can't be happening.

She made a sound into his mouth that was more like a moan, and he responded by cupping her breast and moving his hips against hers. She felt an intense sudden urge to wind her arms around his neck and pull him closer. An ache spread through her belly into her thighs.

She knew she had to stop.

Immediately.

She pressed her palms more firmly against his broad hard chest and pushed. He paid no attention. His lips left her mouth and moved down her throat leaving hot, wet kisses.

"Jared," she finally managed, but her raspy voice sounded more like encouragement than an objection. He must have thought so, too, because he pulled her tighter against him, cupping her buttocks as he moved against the juncture of her thighs.

He was fully aroused, she realized, and despite her embarrassment, she couldn't deny that she was aroused, as well. His hand moved to the waist of her jeans, and she gasped as he quickly unsnapped the button and started to slide her zipper down.

"Jared!"

In a dim corner of his mind, Jared knew there was a problem with this dream. He just wasn't quite sure what it was. The pleasure pumping through his body at the moment certainly wasn't the problem, and neither was the feel of the soft smooth skin under his fingertips. This was the stuff that real dreams were made of. And since he'd never quite had one this intense before, or this enjoyable, he wasn't quite ready to let go of it yet.

He kept his eyes closed, struggling to hold on to the fantasy—

"Jared!"

A woman called his name again, and he heard the alarm in her voice. This was no dream, he realized abruptly.

Maybe there *was* a problem, after all.

He opened his eyes slowly, waiting for them to adjust to the dim light. There was a woman in bed with him. A living breathing long-limbed woman with short blond hair.

And she sure as hell hadn't been here when he'd gone to bed. He definitely would have remembered, no matter what state he'd been in.

Lifting his head, Jared peered at the woman in the semidarkness. She was breathing rapidly and her breasts were pressed firmly against his chest. The hardened peaks of her nipples burned his skin. He could feel the furious beating of her heart and realized his own heart was keeping time.

Dammit. The woman in his dream had not only been willing, she'd been eager. This woman was obviously distressed, and the pressure she exerted on his shoulders was hardly an invitation to lovemaking.

"Who are you?" he said raggedly. "And what the hell are you doing here?"

"Jared, it's Annie," she said breathlessly. "Annie Bailey."

He went completely still. He blinked, then sucked in a deep breath. "What?"

"Annie Bailey," she repeated.

Jared frowned deeply, drawing his dark brows together.

"Annie?" Bewildered, he lifted his head higher, blinking again as his eyes began to adjust to the light and focus on the woman lying beneath him. "Annie... *Bailey?*"

She nodded.

They both lay there, breathing hard, neither one of them moving, whether to hold on to the contact or because they were both too stunned to move, Jared wasn't sure. He stared at her, absorbing the fact that she was not only real, but she was in his bed.

And one of them wasn't wearing any clothes.

He rolled away from her, swearing as he grabbed the covers and pulled them over his hips. Annie sat, turning her back to him, and he watched as she took a few deep breaths.

He narrowed his eyes. It *was* Annie. Her hair was shorter, but she most definitely was Jonathan's fiancée.

Ex-fiancée, Jared reminded himself grimly.

Her eyes were wide and full of expression as she turned back to him. "Hello, Jared," she said, smiling weakly as she forced a short laugh. "It's, uh, nice to see you."

He frowned at her. She certainly *had* seen him. That was like Annie, to try to alleviate tension with a joke. The only problem was, he wasn't exactly in a joking mood at the moment.

He was still reeling with the realization that he'd woken up with a woman in his bed. That hadn't happened in a hell of a long time. And it wasn't just *any* woman. It was *Annie,* for God's sake.

He closed his eyes and drew in a deep breath, still trying to bring his body under control. He'd been dreaming something incredibly erotic. Although that certainly wasn't strange, considering the state of his sex life lately. The woman in his dream had been tall and slender and blond, and while that wasn't strange, either, the fact that she'd looked remarkably like Annie was. He still wasn't sure exactly what *had* happened, but he did know that he'd nearly made love to her, that he sure as hell had *wanted* to.

Dammit. He *still* wanted to.

His throat suddenly felt dry as a Texas plain. He stared at the bottle beside the bed and realized he'd probably had a little too much last night. He did that occasionally. Sometimes he had weird dreams.

But Annie had been no dream. She was very real, and sitting twelve inches away from him.

He couldn't stop the ache that tightened his loins. Damn, but she had felt good. She'd smelled like spring flowers and tasted like something minty. Her skin had felt soft and smooth under his hands, and her hardened nipple under his palm—

He cursed himself again. This was *Annie*. Jonathan's Annie. He couldn't think about her like that. He had no right.

He'd never have that right.

He raked a hand through his tousled hair and closed his eyes. "Annie ... God, I'm sorry. I didn't realize."

"Hey, Jared, it's okay," she said with a flip of her hand, but he could see her fingers shake as she tucked a loose strand of blond hair behind one ear.

Dammit, she had every right to be scared. He'd practically attacked her!

"Besides," she went on, "it's my fault. I never should have come in here like I did. It's just that I heard a crash and you called out, and I, well, I thought you were sick or something."

A crash? Jared glanced around the room, then realized that a glass, the one that had been sitting beside the whiskey bottle, had fallen behind the nightstand and shattered. Good Lord, had he been reaching for the bottle even in his sleep?

"I'm fine." Careful to keep his distance from her and just as careful to keep the sheet over his hips, Jared scooted to the edge of the bed. "I had a late night, that's all."

It must have been later than he thought, Jared realized, as he searched the bedroom floor. "Where the hell are my pants?" he mumbled irritably to himself.

"There's a pair of jeans in the living room," Annie said awkwardly. "They're wet, though."

Jared frowned. He'd been outside on the steps, and it had started raining. He'd obviously stayed out longer than good sense dictated.

But then, good sense was hardly one of his strong points, he reminded himself, in light of what had just happened.

He stood, intending to grab a dry pair of jeans from his dresser, then remembered his state of undress. When he quickly sat back down, she looked away and started to rise.

"I . . . uh, I'll just wait for you in the other room."

"No." He took hold of her wrist and gently tugged her back down. Her pulse beat hard and fast under his fingertips.

He knew he should ask her to leave, but for some strange reason, he didn't want her to go. Not just yet, anyway. Maybe because after nearly four years it was easier to face her here in the darkness, or maybe it was because he still didn't want to face reality. He wasn't sure what the reason was, but he did know that, even if it was only a few more minutes, he wanted her to stay right where she was.

"Just grab a pair of jeans out of that top drawer for me." He gestured toward his dresser.

"Sure." She stood and opened the drawer, then handed him the jeans. She folded her arms and looked away as he tugged the pants on.

When Annie felt brave enough to chance a look at him again, she was relieved to see that he was at least partially dressed. It was difficult enough standing here talking to him, pretending nonchalance, after what had just transpired between them. Her knees were the consistency of dry sand and her cheeks burned with embarrassment. Thank God the room was dark, she thought. She wasn't quite sure how she could look Jared directly in the eyes at the moment, let alone have a calm conversation with him in the light of day.

He reached across her and pulled a T-shirt out of the dresser. She watched as he dragged it over his head, and it was impossible not to notice the ripple of lean hard muscle as he tugged it on. Goodness, but the Stone men were well built, she noted, quickly looking away.

Extremely well built.

"I—" she drew in a deep breath "—I just heard about your father. I'm sorry. I would have come for the funeral if I'd known."

Jared tucked his T-shirt into his jeans, and Annie's throat tightened as he pulled up the zipper. "Myrna made all the arrangements so fast even *I* couldn't make it in time. I barely made it to the reading of the will."

Annie remembered Jared's stepmother. An attractive woman with red hair, she'd been somewhere in her late forties when Annie had last seen her. J.T. had married the woman close to twelve years ago, one year after Jonathan and Jared's mother had died. Annie knew that Myrna was more tolerated by the Stone children than accepted.

Jared's head snapped up suddenly and he looked at the lighted clock on the nightstand. His eyes widened. "Dammit. Dammit, *dammit!*"

"What?" Eyes wide, Annie stared at Jared. "What is it?"

He snatched a pair of socks from his dresser, then grabbed his boots. "I've got an appointment. Jeez, I *had* an appointment. At ten with a geologist from Arloco Oil. I was supposed to meet him at the rig. Annie, I'm sorry, but I have to go. If I blow this appointment, it will undoubtably put an end to my already shaky oil career."

He hesitated at the bedroom door and ran a hand quickly through his hair. "Look, just make yourself comfortable. I'll be back in—"

"Jared—"

"—a little while and—"

"Jared—"

"—we can talk then about—"

"Jared!"

He stopped. "What?"

"Jared, I hate to tell you this." She swallowed hard and faced him. "But I'm your geologist."

Two

Jared stared at Annie, certain he had misunderstood her. She *couldn't* mean what he thought she meant.

"What did you say?"

"I said," she repeated quietly, "I'm your geologist. The one you were supposed to meet this morning."

An uneasiness tightened Jared's chest. "From Arloco Oil?"

"Yes."

No. She couldn't be. Not *Annie.* He reached for the light switch and flipped it on. She blinked at the unexpected brightness.

Annie *had* been a geology major, Jared remembered. That was how she and Jonathan had met. He had just finished his last year when they'd become engaged, but she'd had one more year before she graduated.

He watched her, letting the impact of her words sink in.

"So this is no social call," he said carefully. "You're here as a representative of Arloco Oil."

She nodded. "That's right."

He took in the full sight of her: work boots, long denim-clad legs, white sleeveless blouse, short tousled blond hair, large hazel eyes and wide soft lips.

Lips that were still swollen from the kiss he'd unknowingly forced on her.

The uneasiness in his chest closed around him like a fist. He'd more than blown his chances with Arloco Oil. He'd pulverized them.

He stared down at his bare feet, then back to her. "Look, just give me a minute. You've caught me a little off guard here."

She smiled weakly. "You might say the same thing for me."

He rolled his eyes shut and groaned. "Annie, I'm sorry, I—"

She cut him off. "Never mind, Jared. Let's just forget about it. There was no harm done. We'll laugh about it later."

He seriously doubted that. Nor did he think he'd forget about it, either.

"I'll go put some coffee on," she offered as casually as if she'd been gone four days, instead of almost four years. "I'll meet you in the kitchen, and we'll start all over. It should help," she added with a smile, "that we'll both be dressed this time."

He could hear the teasing in her voice, but he was hardly in the mood for levity. Frowning, he stepped aside, wondering how a day that had started off feeling so damn good could end up so damn miserable.

Annie held her breath as she moved past Jared. The look on his face told her that he hadn't appreciated her weak attempt to ease the tension between them. She sighed inwardly. She'd known it was going to be difficult seeing Jared after all these years, but she certainly hadn't expected it to be quite *this* difficult.

Everything in the kitchen was pretty much in the same place as when Jonathan had lived here, and she had a pot of coffee brewing within a couple of minutes. When she opened the cabinet where she remembered the cups had been, an image of Jonathan reaching into this same cupboard suddenly came to her. He'd made dinner for her the night he'd proposed, a romantic candlelight meal with wine and flowers. When he'd slipped the ring on her finger, she knew she was the luckiest woman alive.

Strange, she thought, staring at the plastic coffee mugs in her hand, how quickly and how cruelly happiness can be snatched away.

"Annie?"

Startled, she turned abruptly and dropped one of the mugs. It bounced on the tile of the kitchen floor, then landed on the living-room floor.

"I—I'm sorry," she gasped, scrambling after the cup. Jared reached for it at the same time, and their fingers touched. She quickly pulled hers away, and they both straightened.

This time, when his gaze met hers, he smiled. "No harm done," he said, mimicking the words she'd used earlier.

He took the other mug from her and moved to the coffeepot. It was still sputtering and bubbling, but he filled the cups anyway. The hot liquid dripped and sizzled on the burner.

She took a calming breath, watching as Jared poured the steaming coffee. He'd combed his hair, and the thick dark ends brushed the back of his neck. He looked the same physically as he had four years ago, except his arms and shoulders appeared more muscular than she remembered. He was almost a foot taller than her own five-foot-four frame, and she had to look up to meet his eyes when he turned and offered her a cup. They were the same deep blue as Jonathan's had been. Stone blue, she'd called it, since all the Stone children had the same incredible eye color. It reminded her of the ocean at sunrise.

He handed her a mug. "Black all right?"

"Fine." She accepted the cup, thankful to have something to hold on to.

"Annie—"

She raised a hand to stop him. "Jared, please, before we get to business, can we just talk a little? Maybe catch up on a few things?"

He stared at her over his coffee cup for a long moment, then leaned back against the counter. "All right."

They both stood there.

She cleared her throat. "So how are you?"

What an inane thing to say. Blast it! Why was this so difficult?

He just nodded. "Okay. You?"

She nodded, too. "Fine."

He sipped his coffee, watching her, and Annie felt a heat scurry through her at the intensity of his gaze.

"You look different," he said at last.

He didn't, she thought. He was as handsome as she remembered. Jonathan's good looks had been more refined somehow, while Jared had been more rugged. "It *has* been almost four years."

His gaze skimmed over her face. "Your hair."

Embarrassed, she ran a hand through her newly cropped hair, suddenly wishing she hadn't let the stylist talk her into the shorter cut. She'd nearly cried when she'd seen six inches of blond hair lying on the floor. "It's supposed to be easier," she said self-consciously.

The corners of his mouth tilted up slightly. "I like it."

She thought she was in control again, but her cheeks suddenly felt warm. She blew away the steam rising from the cup in her hand, then took a sip of the hot liquid. "I heard you were in Venezuela."

His lips thinned. "I was."

Wrong subject, Annie, she thought with a silent groan. From the hard expression on Jared's face, she guessed that South America hadn't exactly been a picnic. It was also perfectly clear that he didn't want to talk about it.

Jared's reticence seemed to be another area where he and Jonathan had differed. Annie had never met anyone more open and verbal than Jonathan had been. Something told her that it would take a crowbar to extract anything more than superficial conversation out of Jared.

"Jake and Jessica?" she inquired about his sister and brother, intentionally changing the subject.

Jared's smile returned, and she couldn't help but notice the attractive lift of his dark eyebrows. "Jessica's living in town. She's applying for a grant so she can turn the ghost town she inherited into a camp for troubled kids."

"Ghost town?"

Jared laughed. "I'll let her tell you about it when she gets back from San Antonio. Jake and his wife, Savannah, took Emma to the Fall Festival there and she went with them."

"Jake married! So there *are* snowballs in hell, huh?" she joked, remembering a remark Jared's older brother had repeated more than once in the short time she'd known him. He'd been recently divorced back then and the subject of marriage was not his favorite. "And who's Emma?"

"My half sister." He chuckled at her confused stare. "It's a long story. I'll explain everything later."

Obviously a lot had transpired since she'd last seen the Stones, Annie thought in amazement. A great number of changes had taken place with the family. Except for one thing.

The oil well.

Which brought her back to why she was here.

The lightness she'd felt a moment ago was gone now. In its place was an ache that settled over her like a lead weight.

The silence stretched around them as taut and thin as a spider's web. If she touched one delicate strand, the entire web would either fall apart or ensnare her. Either way, someone lost.

As if sensing her plight, Jared made the first move. "How long have you worked for Arloco?"

"Almost two years. My first few months out of school I worked for a major oil company, mostly desk work. It's not easy being a woman in a male-dominated industry, but I suppose being the youngest and only daughter of six children was a good training ground. When Arloco offered me a job, I jumped at the opportunity to work in the field for an independent company." She made a small gesture with her hand. "So here I am."

So here she was.

The awkwardness was back between them.

"Look, Annie," Jared said, pushing away from the counter, "this is difficult for both of us. There's a lot of…history here. It might be easier if we put that book on the shelf and just deal with the present. You don't know me, I don't know you. You're here to do a job. Just do it."

She lifted her gaze to his. His eyes were narrowed, his lips drawn tightly together. He was right, of course. This was business, no matter what the past.

"Jared," she said carefully, "you know that after I review everything here I have to draw up a report."

"And based on your report, Arloco either gives or doesn't give its support."

It was bad enough, knowing that she was the one person who could destroy his dream, but hearing him speak the words made her stomach twist into a knot.

Her hands tightened around the cup. "I wish it wasn't me standing here, Jared. But it is. This is my job. I can't compromise that."

"I didn't ask you to," he said tightly. "Nor do I expect it. Just give the project a chance."

She hadn't meant to offend him. This whole situation was just so difficult. She was walking on eggshells here, and none too lightly. "You have the maps?"

"They're in my office." He gestured toward the living room. "Why don't we step in there?"

The teasing lilt was back again and she relaxed a bit. She appreciated that he was at least trying to make it easier for her. With a sigh, she moved past him, determined to put her mind to her work.

Annie sat cross-legged on the floor, a log sheet in one hand and a pencil in the other. She stared at the map spread out on the floor in front of her, her concentration intense as she cross-referenced the map to the logs.

On the floor beside her, Jared took a sip of his fifth cup of coffee as he watched her lean forward, her eyes narrowed, and study the sketched-out cross section of a trap fault. When her hair fell across her cheek, she unconsciously tucked it behind her ear with a smooth flick of her fingers.

She'd changed a lot since he'd first met her, he noted. Her blond hair had been halfway down her back before, and straight. Now it sort of curved around her oval face, accentuating her large hazel-green eyes and thick dark lashes. The style also revealed the long slender line of her neck. In a dim recess of his mind, he had an image of his lips pressed against that soft sensitive spot just below her ear. He cursed himself and tore his gaze away, determined to put the morning's incident between them out of his thoughts.

The sound of her scribbling in the notepad at her knee brought his attention back to the present. It was almost as if she'd forgotten he was there. For the past three hours, she'd pored over the map that Jonathan had worked up— a "play," it was called—and occasionally she'd ask a question, but there'd been virtually no conversation between them. It was starting to grate on his nerves, not knowing what was going on in her head.

He almost laughed at that. As if he'd ever known what went on in any female's head.

He remembered the day Jonathan had brought her home. She'd looked like a typical college student. A long-legged long-haired blonde who would have turned any man's head.

But now there was something more, something provocative, even seductive, in the way she spoke and moved. It made no difference she was wearing work boots and jeans and a loose-fitting white blouse. The femininity that radiated from her packed a punch with definite knockout power.

And when she began to nibble on the eraser of her pencil, Jared's mouth went as dry as chalk. No matter how hard he tried, he couldn't forget the feel of those soft lips under his own. Or the feel of her body pressed tightly against his.

"Jared," she said suddenly, and he nearly jumped at the sound of his name, "did you have a seismic crew out here three years ago?"

He nodded. "I've got the file at the site."

As she stared at the log sheet in her hand, then the map, she frowned slightly. Jared wasn't at all sure he cared for the expression. He'd seen it too many times on bank officers and backers not to recognize it. It meant doubt. With a capital D.

He heard her stomach rumble then and realized that he hadn't offered her anything to eat. Her cheeks flushed as she pressed a hand to her stomach.

He really knew how to rack up points, Jared thought sourly. First he attacked the woman, then he starved her.

"I'll throw some lunch together," he said, standing.

"I am a little hungry," she admitted, tucking the pencil behind her ear and stretching. "I left Midland this morning about seven and didn't take the time to pull off at a diner for breakfast."

"Sandwiches—" He stopped abruptly at the sight of Annie's full breasts pressing tightly against her blouse as she arched her back and groaned. He quickly recovered, though he had to swallow first in order to finish speaking. "—are about the extent of my culinary abilities."

"Really?" She gave him a curious look. "I would have thought that—"

She caught herself, but he knew what she'd been about to say. Jonathan had practically been a gourmet cook. Jared felt a strange surge of anger and nearly blurted out that he wasn't Jonathan, but he held his words in check.

"I manage to get by on canned soup and frozen dinners," he said, moving into the kitchen. "Jessica takes pity on me once in a while and cooks something for me. Even Savannah insists I come over for dinner at least once a week."

He opened the refrigerator and loaded his arms with sandwich makings, then shut the door and plopped everything down on the counter. "I must look like I'm wasting away, the way they fuss over me."

Hardly, Annie thought, uncrossing her legs and standing. In fact, she doubted she'd ever seen a healthier more virile man than Jared.

And she certainly had *seen* Jared.

For the most part, she'd managed not to think about what had happened between them this morning. There'd been momentary lapses, such as when he'd spoken and the rough grain of his voice had skimmed over her skin like a current of low-voltage electricity. Or the time he'd brushed her knee with his, and her heart had shifted into double time. The idea of women fussing over Jared was not a difficult concept to grasp.

She sat on a bar stool opposite him at the counter, watching him slice a tomato with a sharp knife. His hands fascinated her. They were large, with long work-worn fingers and callused palms. She'd experienced their rough texture on her skin that morning and knew firsthand the sensuality they contained.

She knew the pleasure they contained, as well.

"Lettuce?" he asked.

"Please." Disturbed by her thoughts, she looked quickly away, pretending interest in a small clay paperweight shaped like an oil well.

What was happening here? she asked herself, lifting the paperweight so she'd have something to occupy her hands. She *couldn't* be attracted to Jared. He was Jonathan's brother.

Since Jonathan, she hadn't found anyone who had interested her enough to date more than casually. Most of the men she met in the field were arrogant die-hard chauvinists whose main hobby was seeing how quickly they could get a woman into the sack.

She couldn't help the smile that crept over her lips. Jared had probably beat the world record this morning in that masculine sport.

"Emma made it for me."

"What?" She glanced up sharply.

"The paperweight." He gestured to the crude sculpture in her hands. "Emma made it."

"Emma?" Annie turned it over and noticed the inscription on the bottom: *To Jared. E.R.S.* "Oh, yes. Your half sister. You want to tell me about her?"

He handed Annie a sandwich. "We found out about her at the reading of J.T.'s will. Turns out that my father had an affair ten years ago with the architect who designed his house."

"You mean Stone Manor?" Annie asked, remembering the huge house that J.T.'s wife, Myrna Stone, had been so proud of and lived in still. Annie had never liked the place. It was cold and pretentious, like the woman herself.

Jared nodded. "The architect's name was Angela Roberts. She left when she found out she was pregnant. She never told my father, and it was several years before he finally hired a private investigator to look for her. The man managed to uncover the fact that Angela had had a baby, but unfortunately J.T. died before the mother or child could be found."

Annie started to take a bite of her sandwich, then stopped. "But... then, how did you, I mean..."

Jared reached behind him and opened the refrigerator. He pulled out two sodas and set one in front of Annie.

"Jake continued the search. The P.I. found the child five months later. Only problem—" he popped the lid of his soda and it fizzed loudly "—was that Angela Roberts had also died."

Annie closed her eyes and released a long slow breath. "Oh, Jared, I'm so sorry."

He stared at the soda can for a long moment, then nodded grimly.

"Anyway," Jared continued, "when we found Emma a few months ago she was living with an aunt. It wasn't easy, but Jake talked the aunt into coming here with Emma for a visit." A smile lifted one corner of Jared's mouth. "Then he married her."

Annie still couldn't believe it. Jake, of all people, remarried. She remembered that when Jonathan had told Jake he was getting married, the first thing Jake had said was, "Better you than me, bro. Have a dozen kids to make up for the ones I won't." Though he'd laughed as he said it, the smile never made it to his eyes.

The sandwich she was eating suddenly tasted like sawdust in her mouth. Annie had never had the chance to even marry Jonathan, let alone have his children. She'd almost thought—even hoped—that she'd been pregnant when she'd left that summer. She'd desperately wanted something of Jonathan she could have with her always, a part of him that she could love. A child.

But she hadn't been pregnant. She realized later, of course, that it was for the best, but at the time she'd been disappointed.

She set the sandwich down and looked at Jared. "And now you're here, too."

"And now I'm here."

And so am I, she thought.

For a few minutes there'd been an easiness between them, a connection that surprised her. But it was gone now, as if it were no more than a wisp of smoke.

And they were both abruptly aware that her visit was not of a social nature.

A weariness overcame her, and she felt a sudden desperate need to be alone. Away from here. She stood and rolled her shoulder to loosen the stiffness there.

"Thanks for the sandwich, Jared, but I think I've done all I'm capable of doing for now. I'm beat. It's been a long drive here from Dallas. Why don't we start fresh tomorrow and take a look at the rig first thing in the morning? Say about nine?"

"All right." He set his sandwich down as if he, too, had lost his appetite. "Where are you staying?"

Annie couldn't help but notice the fatigue that lined the edges of his deep blue eyes, and she realized that he was just as tired as she was. Based on the condition she'd found him in this morning, she assumed he hadn't slept much the night before. She'd also noticed that he hadn't stepped too close to a razor for a couple of days, and unbidden, the memory of how those rough bristles had felt against her neck flooded her mind.

She looked away, letting her insides settle before trusting herself to speak.

"I have a room in town," she said, turning around and gathering up her notes. "At the Cactus Flat Motel. You can call me there if you need to. I'll be going over this paperwork tonight."

She turned to leave, then turned back again and lifted her gaze to his. "I know it's hard for you, my being here," she said quietly. "I'm sorry."

He nodded slowly, and she saw the pain in his eyes as he stared at her. The most natural thing in the world would have been to go to him and put her arms around him. To comfort him and to be comforted.

But she didn't. And though she didn't know why, she did know that in all the time she'd been here neither she nor Jared had said Jonathan's name once.

Three

—

Annie was already at the rig when Jared drove up the next morning. At least her car was there, he noted as he pulled up beside the Cherokee, but she wasn't in it.

He'd arrived early, hoping to get there before her. Partly to give himself a few minutes to do a test run on the drill motor, and partly because he needed a few minutes alone there before she showed up.

Maybe she'd needed a few minutes herself, Jared realized grimly.

He stepped out of his truck and tipped his Stetson back as he searched the area. The equipment shed was locked, so she couldn't be in there. He started toward the small square trailer that served as office and lounge for the crew, but hadn't gotten more than a few feet when he heard her call his name. Turning, he frowned as he looked around, but still didn't see her.

"Good morning."

Glancing upward, he narrowed his eyes and focused on a slender form silhouetted by the rising sun. She stood at the edge of the derrick platform twenty-five feet off the ground, her hand lifted in a wave.

He froze.

He couldn't breathe. His heart pounded with bruising force against his ribs. He wanted to scream at her to move back, to get away from the edge, but his voice had suddenly gone numb.

"Jared?" she called down, and stepped even closer to the edge. "Are you all right?"

His hands were shaking now. He clenched them into fists and, without taking his eyes off her, walked stiffly to the metal platform steps, then moved slowly upward toward her. At the top of the stairs, he paused, his jaw tight, and stared at her.

Brow furrowed, Annie asked, "Is something wrong?"

As she stepped away from the ledge, the steel band around Jared's chest loosened and he could breathe again. "What the hell are you doing up here?"

"Waiting for you."

"You haven't got any gear on," he said more sharply than he intended. He was still waiting for his heart to slow down, trying not to think about how close she'd been to the edge....

"Gear?" She frowned at him. "Jared, for heaven's sake, I'm just looking around."

"There's no place on a rig for sight-seeing, Annie. You want a tour, take the bus." He knew he was being unreasonable, but he didn't care. "Next time you come up here, you better have a damn good reason, and you better be wearing a safety belt and hat."

"A hat!" She stared at him incredulously. "You're not even drilling yet."

"That would have made me feel loads better if I'd driven up and found you in a dozen pieces. And now that I think about it, you don't need to be up here at all. You need something, let me or one of my crew handle it for you."

She moved close to him, close enough that he could see the flecks of green sparkle in her hazel eyes, close enough that he could smell the flowery scent of her skin. He wanted to move away, but he held his ground.

"I've been in the field now for almost two years." She tilted her chin upward. "I've been on a dozen rigs like this. I know what I'm doing."

Don't worry about me. I know what I'm doing....

How many times had he awakened in the middle of the night, drenched with sweat, with those words pounding in his head?

He couldn't take that chance again. Not with Annie. "I don't want you up here."

She stared at him in disbelief. "You can't be serious."

"Damn straight I am. You have no reason to be up on the rig."

Her mouth thinned, and he felt his gut tighten as he stared at her lips and remembered how soft they'd felt under his, how warm. He quickly pushed the thought aside.

"Jared, I know what's bothering you, and it's understandable, but I have a job to do here."

"Your job," he said tightly, "involves the logging and mapping and soil samples. Once I've hired my crew, we'll take care of everything else."

She shook her head. "That's not my style. I know most geologists keep their distance, but my policy is strictly hands-on."

He tried to ward off the impulse to throw her over his shoulder and carry her off the rig. "I set the policies around here. I'm responsible for three crews of six men twenty-four hours a day. I won't be responsible for you, too."

Her eyes flashed with anger. "*Responsible* for me? Of all the—" She leveled her gaze on his. "Jared, sit down."

"What?"

"I said, sit down." She pointed to the floor of the platform.

He narrowed his eyes, then did as she asked, stretching one leg out in front of him and bending the other. She sat facing him, curling her legs under her in a way that made him think about how long and slender those limbs were in her tight jeans.

She laced her fingers together and stared at them for a long moment. A hawk swept close to the derrick, screeching as it soared past, and a prairie dog chattered a warning to the underground community that a predator was close by.

He waited for her to speak, watching as a breeze ruffled the ends of her hair. She combed the loose strands away from her face and finally lifted her gaze to his. Her eyes were soft now, edged with a sadness that twisted his insides.

He understood with painful clarity how his brother had fallen in love with this woman. And he also understood why he had to keep his distance.

"Jared." She reached out and laid her hands on his. "It wasn't your fault."

His jaw clenched as he stared down at her fingers resting on his knuckles. Her skin was smooth and cool, yet her touch burned. But he didn't want her understanding. And he sure as hell didn't want her pity. "So I've been told."

She frowned and her fingers closed around his. "Dammit, Jared, it *wasn't* your fault. It was an accident. A terrible tragic accident. There was nothing you could have done to prevent it.''

"He didn't belong up here," Jared said tightly. "He wasn't familiar with the operation yet. He didn't have the experience.''

"And you think you could have stopped him?''

It was a question he'd asked himself every day for almost four years. A question he'd never have an answer to. "I should have insisted. He didn't understand the risks.''

She shook her head. "He understood more than you give him credit for. The need to be a part of it, every aspect of it, was in his blood just as strongly as it was—and still is—in yours. You couldn't have taken that away from him.''

Jared stared at Annie, amazed at the compassion lighting her face. She'd lost her future with the man she'd loved, yet she sat here and attempted to comfort him. Anger at himself, as hot as it was black, shot through him. "I was the one with working experience on this rig. Jonathan was green, right out of the classroom.''

Annie felt Jared's hands tighten beneath her touch. His jaw was taut, and his eyes . . . Lord, the pain she saw there was like a sharp knife twisting in her chest. She drew in a slow ragged breath and forced herself to hold his gaze with her own.

"Do you realize," she asked quietly, "that's the first time you've even said his name?''

His lips thinned and he looked away, but for one split second, so brief she almost thought she imagined it, Annie saw—and understood—the depth of Jared's anguish. The first year after Jonathan's death, she'd seen that same look staring back at her from the mirror. She'd felt that grief. She'd lived it. Time had slowly healed her, but Jared, apparently, hadn't been so fortunate.

She felt a desperate need to free him from his torment, to ease the pain he'd lived with for the past several years. But what could she say? What could she do? Jared wasn't going to let anyone get that close. The wall he'd built around himself served not only to keep everyone else out, but to keep him in, as well. And of all the people he didn't want help from, Annie was first on the list, she knew. If anything, Jared wanted her as far away from him as possible.

Because she couldn't stop herself, she leaned in closer and stroked the back of his hands with her thumbs. The coarse texture of his skin amazed her, but not nearly as much as the moisture that gathered in her eyes and fell onto Jared's fingers. Was she crying for Jonathan or for Jared?

Dammit, Jared thought. Not tears. He could stand anything but tears. He reached for her then and pulled her into his arms, cradling her body against his. "Aw, jeez, Annie, don't cry. Please don't cry."

"I'm not," she insisted with a sniff. "Not really."

He smiled as she wiped at her eyes, but when she laid her head against his shoulder his smile faded.

A heat began to build in him. Even though he'd been half-asleep when he'd kissed Annie yesterday, he'd never forget the taste of her. The sweetness, and the shimmer of innocence that had made his blood race and his pulse pound.

Her cheek brushed his neck, and the warmth of her sigh on his skin had his blood pounding again, only faster and more furious this time because he was wide awake now and more aware of Annie in his arms than he had ever been aware of any woman in his entire life.

His hands tightened on her arms, and his mind screamed to move away before she felt his arousal. But somehow he

was pulling her closer, tucking her against him as if he
might never let go.

"Annie," he breathed her name with a ragged whisper,
"I—"

He stopped himself. *I what? I want you? I need you?*
For God's sake! This was *Annie.* Jonathan's Annie. He
didn't have the right. Not ever.

With willpower he didn't know he possessed, he finally
set her away from him. He struggled to breathe, and when
he looked at her flushed face and saw the confusion in her
eyes, he decided that horse whipping wouldn't be good
enough for him. She'd needed comfort and he'd wanted to
take her. To touch her and make love to her. Right here.
Right where Jonathan had died.

Disgusted with himself, he stood and pulled her to her
feet. "You might want to take a look at the equipment,"
he said in a voice that sounded foreign to him. "It was
purchased new three years ago, and I've reconditioned
everything in the past few weeks."

Annie felt as if everything inside her was shifting. She
looked at Jared, heard him speaking, but she hadn't a clue
what he'd said. Her heart beat low and heavy. Her throat
felt dry. When he let go of her hand, she nearly protested.

What had just happened between them? Something very
strong, powerful even. It had the same physical drive as
yesterday when he'd pulled her into his bed and kissed her,
but there was an even stronger force this time, something
that went beyond attraction. Something primitive and raw,
a need that shook her clear to her toes.

Her pulse increased as he watched her with eyes that
were as dark as they were intense. They stood mere inches
from each other. A simple lift of a hand would connect
them, bring them together. Her body tingled with anticipation.

"Jared—"

The blast of a car horn shattered the moment like fragile glass. Annie turned and watched the approach of a white luxury sedan. Clouds of dust billowed behind the car as it turned off the paved road and made its way toward them.

Jared stepped away from her and tipped back his hat. "The woman is determined, I'll give her that much."

Annie looked at him curiously. "What woman?"

"Myrna."

"Your stepmother?"

Jared nodded, watching the sedan approach. "Ever since she realized she couldn't buy Jake's land, she's been after mine. She makes at least a weekly trip out here."

He sighed, then turned and headed for the stairs. Annie followed, hurrying to keep up with Jared's long strides. "Why would she want to buy this land? Is she interested in drilling for oil?"

His laugh was dry and harsh. "Hardly. She's got this idea she wants to breed and train Thoroughbreds."

"Horses? Myrna?" Annie couldn't keep the surprise from her voice. The Myrna that Annie remembered hated horses. She'd hated the smell and the flies and the "stable refuse," as she'd so fondly referred to the ever-present mountains of manure.

"It's a real hoot, ain't it?" Jared waited at the base of the stairs, his gaze narrowed as the cloud of dust grew closer. "Not that she'd ever spend a penny of her own money. She's managed to convince Carlton to buy it for her."

"Carlton?"

"Her father. Carlton Hewitt III. He's never said no to the woman once in her life. I always thought she married my father because he was the first man who ever did say no." Jared's expression was somber as he leaned back against a rig post and folded his arms across his chest. "But even that changed after they'd been married for a while. She built that damn house of hers and spent every penny of J.T.'s money she could get her hands on. He stood by and never said a word."

Annie watched the sedan pull up in front of the office trailer. "Why?"

"I suspect it had to do with Angela. He wasn't the same man after she left." Jared shook his head. "He just sort of gave up."

"Until he found out he had another daughter," Annie said quietly.

"We found out last month that Myrna knew all along. Not only about the affair, but that Angela was pregnant." Jared's jaw tightened. "I can forgive her a lot of things, but not that. Emma is our sister, our blood, and we all missed out on a lot of years."

Annie touched Jared's arm. "But you have her now."

He smiled. "Yeah. We have her now."

The sedan's engine stopped and the car door opened. One white high-heeled shoe touched the dirt, then another. Myrna stepped out of the car, smoothed the front of her yellow skirt, then adjusted her yellow-and-white-striped silk blouse. Her red hair gleamed in the morning sun as brightly as the shiny chrome on her car.

She patted the crisp back of her starched hairdo and headed for the office.

"Over here," Jared called.

Myrna turned abruptly, her hand still poised in midair. "Oh, there you are. I was just on my way to pick Daddy up at the airport and thought I'd stop by to say hello."

As if Myrna ever just stopped to say hello, Jared thought, resisting the urge to roll his eyes. "Your father's coming here?"

"It took a doctor's order to finally get that man to spend some time with me." The woman picked her way toward them, carefully avoiding rocks and shrubs. "He had a couple of dizzy spells, and his physician insisted he take some time off."

Carlton Hewitt coming to Stone Creek was certainly a rare occurrence. If the seventy-three-year-old man wasn't in a business meeting discussing the half of Houston he already owned, he was in a business meeting trying to buy the other half.

Like father, like daughter, Jared noted silently. But maybe while the man was here, it would keep Myrna occupied elsewhere. And for that, Jared would forever be in Carlton's debt.

"Oh, dear me," Myrna said, looking at Annie. "Am I interrupting?"

As if it would matter to her if she was, Jared thought. Before he could answer, his stepmother moved closer to Annie and held out a hand. "Hello, I'm Myrna Stone, Jared's stepmother. You must be the geologist from Arloco that Jared told me about."

Jared ground his teeth. He hadn't told Myrna anything about Arloco or the geologist. She'd obviously been snooping again.

And how could she have forgotten Annie? Myrna had given Jonathan and Annie an engagement party. It was difficult, but Jared held back the swear word on the tip of his tongue.

"Actually we've met, Mrs. Stone," Annie said before Jared could intercede. "I'm Annie Bailey. I was Jonathan's fiancée."

"Annie Bailey?" Myrna's hand froze. She looked at Jared, then back at Annie. "Jonathan's fiancée? But I . . . You mean, you aren't the geologist from Arloco?"

"Well, yes," Annie said. "I'm that, too."

Jared wanted to laugh at the dumbfounded expression on Myrna's face, but even more, he wanted to get rid of the woman.

Myrna moved toward Annie and took her hand. "Annie. Oh, yes, of course I remember you. Jonathan's fiancée. It's just been so long, and I certainly never expected you, of all people, to be Jared's geologist."

"Mrs. Stone," Annie said carefully, "I'm not *Jared's* geologist. I'm here as a representative for Arloco Oil to determine the feasibility of this project."

"Well—" Myrna lifted one perfectly tweezed brow "—Jared must certainly be thankful for that. After all the problems this young man has had finding backers, he must see you as a true godsend." She turned to Jared with a smile as phony as the color of her hair. "I would assume that congratulations are in order."

"Annie is still evaluating the rig," Jared said through clenched teeth. "When she's finished, she'll give her findings to Arloco."

Myrna gestured blithely with her hand. "Well, yes, but she's the one who really decides, doesn't she?"

Jared searched the ground for a rope. He'd tie the woman up, then—

"I have an obligation to Arloco Oil, Mrs. Stone," Annie said tightly. "Whatever decision I make will be based on facts, not emotions."

"Of course it will, dear."

Fingernails on a blackboard would be music compared to the words that came out of Myrna's mouth. Jared spotted a steel cable a few feet away. It was just about the right size—

Myrna faced Annie, oblivious to Jared's murderous thoughts. "It must be so awkward for you, though, considering the circumstances and all." She placed a hand on her chest and looked up. "I mean, working here, right where poor Jonathan fell. How will you ever deal with that?"

Jared felt Annie go rigid beside him. Nothing that Myrna said or did should shock him anymore, but for a second he felt as if he'd been punched in the chest. He also suddenly realized how tightly he was holding on to Annie's arm. He let go and felt her draw in a slow breath, then cursed himself when he saw the imprint of his hand on her smooth skin.

"This is my job, Mrs. Stone," Annie said with a patience that amazed Jared. "My personal feelings have no place here."

Myrna sighed. "Yes, well, I know what it's like to lose someone you love. It's only been eight months since J.T.'s been gone, and I just can't imagine—" her lower lip quivered and she blinked several times "—well, I just loved him so much. I hope someday I'll be able to get over his death as bravely as you have Jonathan's."

That was it. Jared had had enough. He'd just use his bare hands. That would give him more pleasure, anyway. He took a step toward his stepmother. "Myrna—"

Annie laid her hand on Jared's arm. "Bravery has nothing to do with death, Mrs. Stone," she said quietly. "We have no choice but to accept it, no matter how deep or how black the pain. It's also the one thing in life that no one escapes, the one thing that makes us all equal, no matter how different or how special we might think we are."

Annie turned to Jared then, and he saw a tension in her eyes that belied the calm expression on her face. "I still have some questions on cost estimates, Jared. When you're finished here, I'll be in the office." She faced Myrna again and nodded. "Mrs. Stone, it's been a real . . . pleasure."

Eight hours later Annie sat in a booth at the Cactus Motel Café, staring intently at the menu a perky waitress with short platinum hair had thrust into her hands after reciting the nightly specials. The smell of grilled steak and onions wafted deliciously on the air, reminding Annie that she'd forgotten lunch in her hurry to not only finish her report, but to call in a report to the manager at Arloco and ask for verbal authorization for approval.

It was a go.

She'd only heard an hour ago, and the excitement that had been building inside her was bubbling over. Jared would be here any minute, and she couldn't wait to tell him the good news. She'd already ordered wine to celebrate.

Even recalling her run-in with Myrna earlier in the day hadn't dimmed Annie's pleasure. There'd been a cool distant look in Jared's eyes after the woman had finally left that made Annie uneasy. He'd apologized for his stepmother, but Annie had shrugged it off and insisted that whatever the woman said or did had no bearing on the project.

But there had been that one moment, she realized, that one second when she'd looked up at the rig, and doubt had shivered through her. . . .

No. She closed her eyes. No doubts. She could handle this project. She'd put the past behind her, dealt with those ghosts long ago.

But Jared was no ghost. And he wasn't the past. He was the present. And that was where her doubt truly lay.

Her body still hummed from his touch that morning. When she'd laid her hands on his, she'd only meant to reassure, to comfort. Then suddenly he'd been comforting her, and he'd been so close, his body so hot against hers, and she hadn't been able to think about anything else.

She closed her eyes, remembering the heavy beating of his heart, the strength of his broad chest, his hand slowly moving up her arm, and she couldn't help but wonder...

"Annie, you okay?"

Her eyes flew open and she looked into Jared's worried gaze as he slid into the booth across from her. She felt her face burn and reached for her glass, hoping he wouldn't notice her hand was shaking as she took a sip of ice water. "Yes, of course. I'm fine. Just resting my eyes."

He frowned, then lifted a hand to gesture for the waitress. "Annie," he said solemnly, "I would rather not prolong this—"

"Neither would I." Annie leaned forward and smiled brightly. "As of one hour ago, I gave my approval, and Arloco agreed to back you."

The waitress showed up at that moment and set a bottle of red wine and two glasses on the table.

"It's a deal, Jared," she said breathlessly as the waitress filled the glasses, then moved on to another booth. "We can start drilling immediately."

She lifted her glass, waiting for the realization to hit Jared that they were in business. Waiting for him to laugh and lift his glass, too.

He simply stared at her.

"I'm sorry, Annie," he said, his voice tight. "But I'm afraid the deal's off."

Four

Jared's gut twisted as he watched Annie slowly lower her glass.

"What did you say?" she asked very carefully.

"I'm sorry, Annie." Jared wished he had something much stronger than the wine to belt down, though he doubted there was liquor strong enough to erase the look of complete betrayal on Annie's face right now. "I've decided to withdraw my request for backing."

Her fingers tightly clutched the stem of the wineglass. "May I ask why?"

Several more couples had settled into the booths and tables of the restaurant, and the din of conversation mixed with the clatter of busboys and waitresses serving suddenly became deafening. He'd thought it would be easier to tell Annie here, in a public place, that he had changed his mind, but he was wrong. She deserved better than a quick thanks, but no thanks.

He threw several bills on the table, then reached over and took her free hand. Her fingers felt cold and stiff under his own. "Come on."

"But—"

She resisted, but he held tightly and pulled her from the booth. A few curious stares turned their way as he dragged her behind him out the back door of the restaurant into a quiet parking lot. The crescent moon shone brightly overhead, spilling silver light over Annie that danced in her blond hair. She pulled her hand from his and lifted her chin as she glared at him. He noticed for the first time the dress she was wearing. It was black and short, sleeveless, and had a neckline that formed a dangerous V, revealing a swell of soft full curves. His throat went dry. He carefully kept his eyes from that V and focused on her face.

"I've decided that Arloco isn't the right company for me."

"Oh, I see." She arched one delicate brow. "You mean our money isn't quite green enough?"

He frowned. "Dammit, Annie, don't make this any more difficult than it already is."

"And why shouldn't I?" Her eyes flashed in the moonlight. "You seem to forget, you're the one who applied to Arloco. You've wasted my time, and yours, too."

She folded her arms, lifting that enticing swell of flesh ever higher, oblivious to the havoc she was wreaking with his senses. He caught the light floral scent of her perfume that surely was named Come Closer, and it was all he could do not to drag her against him. "Look, I'm sorry. I've decided to go with another company."

She narrowed her eyes in anger. "That's a crock and you know it, Jared. Part of my job is to find out who you've already applied to. Outside of Arloco, the only other company who's considered backing you is Darco Enterprises, and that's only because the president went to college with your father. And even they turned you down.''

Her words were cold and hard, but they were also accurate. ''Gee, Annie,'' he said dryly, ''aim a little higher next time. I may still want to have children one day.''

She ignored him and stepped closer. ''I should just walk out of here, Jared. Arloco has dozens of projects they're interested in. But we have a play here, a strong potential for a sound investment.''

Her eyes searched his face, and he had the distinct feeling that she could see not only through him, but inside him, where no one had before.

''Myrna got to you, didn't she?'' Annie said stiffly.

''Myrna has nothing to do with this.''

''The hell she doesn't. She bruised that male pride of yours when she implied I'd give you Arloco's backing whether the figures panned out or not.''

''Did you?''

Her eyes glinted fiercely. ''As I said to your stepmother, it's been a real pleasure.''

She turned and started to walk away, but his hand snaked out and took hold of her arm. ''Annie,'' he said raggedly, ''I want your backing because you believe in the rig, not because of any obligation you might feel.''

The stiffness eased from her body. ''Jared, this is not an easy business for a woman. It's taken me two years to prove myself with Arloco Oil. I have no intention of breaking the trust they've put in me. Not for you, not for anyone.''

He stared down at her, saw the determination there, the intensity. A pan clanging from the kitchen and a muffled shout for more T-bone steaks were the only sounds to break the silence of the warm night.

"But that isn't the real reason you're backing out," she said, "is it, Jared?"

He said nothing, and she leaned closer to him, her eyes searching his face. "I deserve the truth," she said softly. "You at least owe me that before you slam the door in my face."

He became painfully aware of how smooth her skin felt. Still, he let his hand linger on her arm, resisting the urge to run his fingers up and over the bare curve of her shoulder.

"When I saw you on the rig this morning," he said finally, "standing where Jonathan—"

She closed her fingers over his. "Jared—"

"You wanted the truth. I'm giving it to you. What if something happened to you?"

"Nothing is going to—"

He shook his head and glanced away from her, staring into the shadows of the night. "You don't know that. Accidents happen all the time. You said so yourself. How would I deal with that?"

She touched his cheek and forced him to look at her. "Jared, there are no guarantees in life. But there is something to be lost, something more precious than whatever you might gain, if you don't follow your heart. Jonathan knew that, and I think you do, too."

He did know, dammit. But this was *Annie*. How could he take chances with her? She'd lost so much already. Her fingers moved over his jaw, and he felt the heavy deep thud of his heart. He *couldn't* take that big a risk. He'd walk away from it all before he'd see her hurt again.

"Jared," she said with an urgency that made his heart beat faster, "I never would have given my approval if I hadn't felt this was a viable project. But I also realized something this morning as I stood on the rig. Something that went beyond the numbers and figures and bottom

line. I realized how important this project is to me personally. It's a part of my past that needs to be put to rest. I
want this—for you, for me and for Jonathan. I can't walk
away from it. Don't make me."

A pressure built inside him, a longing of such intensity,
a need so strong, that he felt himself shake under the force
of it. He couldn't do this. He couldn't.

"Please."

One word, spoken softer than the night breeze, and yet
it had the strength of steel chains. He was lost and he knew
it. "I don't want you up on the rig."

One corner of her mouth tilted up. "Unless I absolutely
need to be, I won't."

"And you may be the money, but I call the shots."

The other side of her mouth tilted upward, as well. "Of
course."

His grin came slowly. "Looks like we've got a deal, Miss
Bailey."

"I'd say so, Mr. Stone."

He released her, intending to shake her hand, but then,
with a laugh, she jumped up and circled his neck with her
arms. Startled, he simply stood there, his hands in midair,
not knowing what to do. Her breasts pressed against his
chest, and he sure as hell knew what he *wanted* to do. And
with that dress she was wearing, it would be so damn easy.
He held back the groan deep in his throat.

But he was only human, and it was impossible not to
wrap his arms around her and draw her against him. Just
this one time, he'd allow himself the pleasure of her closeness, of her enthusiasm. He pulled her tightly to him,
breathing in the scent of her as he brushed his lips against
her soft silky hair.

He felt something inside himself shift and settle, a spark
of life he'd thought had died long ago. It wasn't sexual—

though he was certainly feeling that. It was something else, something that scared the hell out of him, because it was something he could never permit himself to feel. Not for Annie.

Because it should be Jonathan standing here with Annie. Jonathan with his arms around this beautiful vibrant woman.

But Jonathan had been cheated out of that happiness, and there was no way Jared would ever allow himself to step in and take his brother's place.

"Now that we have that settled," she said brightly, slipping out of his arms, "can we go eat? I don't know about you, but I'm starving."

She took his hand and he followed her back into the restaurant, afraid to tell her that he was indeed starving. More than she'd ever know.

One week later everything was set in place. The crew—three teams of six men each—was hired, the paperwork completed and the equipment primed and ready to go. Drilling was scheduled to start on Monday and Jared had gone into town to handle the transfer of money from Arloco's bank to his.

Annie leaned forward in the desk chair and stared at the map spread out in front of her. The lines blurred hopelessly together. She'd been here at the site since the crack of dawn, going over the mountains of logs and comparing the figures to the map for the tenth time. The real work hadn't even begun yet, and she was already exhausted.

With a small groan, she stretched and sat back in the chair. For the past week, she'd tossed and turned every night in her motel bed, and her lack of sleep was beginning to wear on her. She tried to tell herself that it was the emotional drain of coming back to Stone Creek, back to the rig where Jonathan had died. But in her heart she knew that wasn't the reason. It had taken a long time, but she'd dealt with those ghosts and laid them to rest.

It was Jared.

Her pulse still skipped every time she remembered the night in the restaurant parking lot. It had been an impulsive act, she knew, throwing her arms around him the way she had. She'd just been so excited at the prospect of reopening the rig she hadn't thought.

But when he'd pulled her into his arms behind the restaurant, she'd known that the fierce beating of her heart had nothing to do with her excitement over the rig. It was a different excitement altogether. It was dark and wild and shimmered between them with the intensity of a live wire. They'd both felt it. They'd both understood. It didn't matter that it was only for a moment. It was strong enough to stun, and frighten, both of them.

He's Jonathan brother, she told herself, then waited for the recriminations. But there were none. Only the lonely sound of goodbyes said long ago. One at the airport, then one over a coffin.

And now fate had brought her back. Back to a place where she'd never thought she'd return, back to the rig that had taken Jonathan from her.

Back to a man who blamed himself for his brother's death.

Sighing, she closed her eyes, wondering what might have happened if she hadn't pulled herself out of Jared's arms the other night. Would he have kissed her? Would it have been a hard demanding kiss, like the first time, or would it have been tender and giving?

He'd been careful to keep his distance the past few days. Almost to the point of being ridiculous. But no matter how much either one of them ignored it, the attraction was still there, hovering, circling. And sooner or later, it was going to come in for a landing. A crash landing, no doubt, she thought with a frown.

"Annie?"

She nearly fell over backward in her chair; her legs flew upward and down as she caught herself. A word no lady should say flew from her lips.

"Jared!" She gripped the chair arm as she spun the seat around to face him. "You startled me."

He grinned at her. "Sorry 'bout that. I thought you heard me drive up."

She might have, if she hadn't been so engrossed in thinking about him. She started to rise from her chair. "No, I—"

She stopped at the sight of another man, in worn jeans and a chambray shirt, standing directly behind Jared. He was a giant of a man, an inch or two taller than Jared, with a barrel chest and short brown hair. A scar cut across his right brow to his temple, and his dark eyes had a narrow dangerous glint in them. She took a deep breath and sank back into her chair.

"Annie," Jared said, "this is Hugh Slater, our fore-man."

Hugh. As in hu-mongous, Annie thought, forcing her legs to push her up and out of the chair. She stuck out her hand, almost expecting to lose it, but when his gigantic paw covered hers, his touch was amazingly gentle. His eyes, a deep brown, took her in, but she sensed that his measure was not of a sexual nature. He was assessing her character.

"What's her fieldwork?" Hugh asked Jared, but kept his eyes on her. He didn't smile.

"Parker Phillips," Jared began, "Sonny Hodges—"

"I can speak for myself, Mr. Slater," Annie said indignantly, and she went on to list the rigs she'd worked on. He was obviously familiar with most of them, because he nodded approvingly several times.

When Annie turned the tables on the man and began to grill him on his experience, Jared sat on the edge of the desk and watched in amusement. Slater's shoulders stiffened and squared as Annie directed several questions at him regarding drilling procedures. People rarely questioned Hugh Slater on his expertise. Especially women.

But then, if Jared had learned anything about Annie, it was only to expect the unexpected. One minute she was sexy and soft and the next minute she was facing down a 250-pound bear of a man without so much as blinking an eye. She had a red pencil stuck behind her ear that seemed to punctuate the air every time she asked a question, while Slater, his massive arms folded, scowled at Annie, answering her with a controlled patience that Jared had never witnessed before.

She was one hell of a woman, he thought. The kind of woman any man would be proud to—

He stopped himself. To what?

To hire, he decided. To have on his team.

He forced his thoughts back to the discussion taking place in front of him. Annie's head was tilted, her brow furrowed, as she listened to Slater explain a complicated but inexpensive method of jetting mud.

Satisfied at last, both Annie and Slater relaxed.

"Welcome aboard, Mr. Slater," Annie said, sticking out her hand again.

"Glad to be here, Miss Bailey." He took her hand. "Just Slater will do."

She nodded. "Bailey for me."

They grinned at each other.

Jared raised an eyebrow at Slater's smile. That was something that happened about as frequently as Halley's comet. If nothing else, Jared noted, it was going to be interesting around here.

"I'd like to take a look at the rig." Slater turned to Jared. "Why don't you join me when you're done in here?"

Jared knew that was Slater's way of asking for a few minutes alone. Jared also understood why. "I'll be out in a while."

Annie stared silently after the big man as he left the office. After a long moment, she sucked in a deep breath and leaned back on the desk beside Jared. "Wow."

He smiled. "That's a common word describing Slater."

"No kidding." She gave her head a shake. "I take it you've worked with him before?"

"Two years in Venezuela."

There was an uneasiness, a tension that Annie suddenly felt from Jared. He was leaving something out, she realized. Then it dawned on her what it was.

"And here?" she asked quietly. "Was Slater the foreman on this rig four years ago?"

His lips thinned. "Yes."

"Was he here, I mean, when..."

"Yes."

She closed her eyes, letting the wave of sadness wash through her. "He wasn't at the funeral."

"Slater doesn't do funerals."

Annie had the distinct feeling that Jared and Slater had been through more than one loss together. She also realized that, whatever it was, it wasn't something Jared wanted to talk about.

Men.

Business was the only thing Jared wanted to talk about, she thought with annoyance. With a sigh, she stood and stared down at the map spread across the desk. "So how did it go in town?"

"Not so well. Three crew members quit."

"Quit!" She glanced up at him. "Why would they do that? You haven't even started drilling yet."

He shook his head. "Said they got a better offer in Odessa. If Slater hadn't brought most of the men with him from Cisco, I probably wouldn't have a crew at all."

"How do you know they won't quit, too?"

"Not Slater's men. I've never seen such loyalty in a crew." He raised a brow. "Would *you* tell Slater you quit?"

She smiled. "No, I guess not." Still, an uneasiness crept through her. "Will you be able to replace the men you lost?"

"Slater's got a few calls out. I have to take him back to town shortly, and we'll see if there's been any response."

"Why don't I take him?" she offered. "I'll be heading that way in a little while, anyway."

Jared's jaw tightened imperceptibly. "Not necessary."

"But it's silly for you to—"

"I said I'd take him."

The sharp edge in Jared's voice made Annie fall silent. His jaw was set, his eyes narrowed as he stared over her shoulder at the map. It didn't make any sense. She knew he had things to do here at the rig, and going back to town was out of his way. If she didn't know better, she could have sworn that he didn't want her to be alone with Slater. But why? Was it possible...? Could he be jealous?

No. She shook the silly thought away. Protective, maybe. But that's all it could be.

But it was there again between them. She felt it building right now. A tension, like a coil being slowly tightened around them. He was a mere hand's width away, and the heat of his body singed her. Her heart lurched in the sudden stillness, and the tension became almost unbearable.

His arm moved up and reached toward her. His eyes darkened to the color of midnight as he stared at her, and she held her breath as he ran his fingertips over her ear. She shivered at the contact, and her eyes drifted closed.

He removed the pencil from her ear.

She jerked her eyes open again, but he'd already bent over the map she'd been working on and was busy scribbling a note.

She wanted to throw something at him. Something large, with sharp edges. Instead, she ground her teeth and counted to ten, then cursed silently. She moved away from him on legs with the consistency of warm molasses.

"By the way," she said coolly, "there're some logs I can't find that Jonathan generated when he worked this map up. Did I leave them in your trailer?"

Jared laid the pencil down and straightened. "They're on my coffee table. I was cross-referencing them to my copy."

She sat back down in the desk chair. "I'll need them to refigure the proposed fault line. Something's not quite right, but I haven't been able to figure out what yet. I'll pick them up on my way back to town tonight."

He nodded, watching her with a quiet intensity that threatened to be her undoing. She looked away from him, forcing her hands to pick up the pencil and turn back to her work.

And when he walked out of the office, she resolved to get—and keep—her mind on business. Even if it killed her.

* * *

Jared parked his truck in front of his trailer and stepped out into the still night air. He stared at the ceiling of stars and raked his hands through his hair. The moon was nearly full, and it cast long shadows over the Texas land, dark lonely shadows that seemed to reach out and close around him.

He had the strangest desire to howl at that moon.

He was bone-tired. He'd had a long week getting everything ready to drill on Monday, and at last it looked as if everything was in place and ready to go. Slater had even managed to find replacements for the men who'd quit.

He grabbed the paper bag off the front seat of his pickup and slammed the door, thankful to be home. What he needed now was a tall stiff drink and a bed.

What he needed now was a woman.

Not just any woman, he acknowledged as he strode toward the trailer door. He could easily have that. Marie Lambert had spotted him at the restaurant where he'd been having dinner with Slater earlier and had slid into the booth beside him. Marie, a beautiful redhead he'd gone to high school with, had made it plain for years that she was interested.

Tonight had been the first time he'd almost taken her up on her unspoken offer. He'd almost convinced himself that taking Marie to bed would ease the ache inside him, the constant burning need that left his temper on high every day and his bed a shambles every night.

But it wasn't a redhead that woke him every night in a cold sweat. It was a blonde. An obstinate determined long-legged blonde with a voice smoother than Southern Comfort and eyes with more shades of gold and green than an autumn meadow.

He'd almost kissed that blonde earlier, when they'd stood so close in the office. His body was still screaming at him because he hadn't. But when he'd run his fingertips over the soft curve of her ear and she'd leaned toward him, her eyes darkening with sensuality, he'd realized that he couldn't. He realized that even the simplest touch, or the simplest kiss, would never be enough.

Annie Bailey was driving him crazy.

With a weary sigh, Jared opened the door to his trailer, dreading another night of endless tossing. He had a full bottle of whiskey, and tomorrow was Saturday. He'd told Annie to take the weekend off, since once they started drilling there would be few breaks. He cradled the paper bag in his arm and thought that maybe, with a little help from his friend here, he could just sleep the weekend away. Once they started drilling, he'd be too distracted and too busy to think about Annie, he told himself.

He made his way to the kitchen in the darkness. The paper bag crinkled as he pulled out the bottle.

He froze.

Turning slowly, he narrowed his eyes and listened intently. A small sound, a sigh, came from the living room. He reached for the kitchen light and flipped it on.

Annie. His throat went dry at the sight of her. She was lying on his couch, her feet dangling over the side, her head propped on a pillow. A map and several logs were spread around her, and he remembered she'd mentioned coming by here.

No. Good Lord, not now. I can't take this.

He looked down at his hand and realized he had the bottle of whiskey in a death grip. He set it down, cursing as he moved toward her. He had to wake her up, get her out of here. *Now.*

He knelt beside her, leaning close as he reached for her shoulder, intending to shake her.

She sighed again, and he felt the soft warmth of her breath on his neck. He squeezed his eyes shut and swallowed hard.

"Annie," he whispered.

She smiled and curled her long slender fingers beside her cheek. Her hair shone like silk.

He cursed again.

His gaze moved slowly over her, at the soft rise and fall of her breasts, the curve of her hip, the long legs in tight jeans. His body responded instantly; he felt the blood pumping through his veins, the pounding of his heart, the growing hardness of his arousal. He imagined what it would be like to slide her clothes off and slip into the heat of her body. To look into her eyes as he moved inside her, to hear his name on her lips, instead of—

He pulled his hand sharply away and stood. He was a fool to allow himself thoughts like that. An idiot.

Because Annie Bailey was the one woman he could never have.

Drawing in a long ragged breath, he moved the map and logs out of the way, then reached for the throw on the arm of the couch and gently covered her with it. She didn't stir.

He moved into the kitchen and frowned at the bottle on the counter. His palms itched, but he left the bottle where it was and shut off the light.

It was going to be a hell of a night.

Five

She awoke slowly, stretching her arms over her head with a satisfied groan. Snuggling under the blanket, she smiled and slipped her arms around the pillow, hugging the soft cushion and sighing contentedly.

Finally a good night's sleep.

She burrowed deeper into the mattress, refusing to open her eyes, even though she was aware that the sun was up. She listened to the quiet tick of a clock and the hum of an air-conditioning unit. The mattress seemed softer this morning, and the smell of coffee was sheer heaven.

The smell of coffee?

She went perfectly still. She hadn't ordered room service. Breath held, she slowly opened her eyes.

Oh, my God.

She was in Jared's living room, on his couch!

She closed her eyes again, praying that she was dreaming, that she hadn't actually spent the night in his trailer.

The last thing she remembered was stopping by here to pick up the logs. She'd sat down to look at Jared's map, then closed her eyes for a moment.

And slept the entire night through.

This time when she ventured a look, she was staring into eyes that were Stone blue. She threw the blanket over her head and groaned again.

"Oh, Jared," she moaned, "why didn't you wake me up?"

She heard him chuckle. "I doubt a herd of horses would have woken you up. And besides, disturbing a peaceful sleep ranks somewhere with kicking puppies and pulling the wings off butterflies."

She pulled the blanket tighter over her head, resisting Jared's tug. She wished the couch would swallow her. "I'm so sorry. I'll get out of your hair as soon as—"

He tugged harder, yanking the blanket off. "Don't worry about it, Annie. It's no big deal."

She peeked up at him, suddenly terribly conscious of what she must look like. But Jared wasn't looking so hot himself, she thought, taking in his tousled hair, dark lines under his eyes and the morning beard. And yet, even though he looked rumpled, he also looked incredibly sexy. He was pure masculinity with his bare broad chest and sleepy eyes. Her pulse responded with a resounding high-speed skip.

Stop it, she told herself. *Don't set yourself up for another fall.*

She sat stiffly, combing the hair away from her face as she struggled to gain some semblance of control. "Are you going to just torture me with that coffee," she said, staring at the cup in his hand, "or are you going to share?"

After the night he'd had, a little torture would be fair measure, Jared thought as he extended the cup toward her.

His bed had looked like a war zone this morning. The image of her soft slender body so close, with only a wall separating them, had driven him crazy. He'd lost count of the times he'd sat on the edge of his mattress, arguing with himself about dragging Annie into his bedroom with him. One time he'd even made it to the door before he came to his senses.

Needless to say, he hadn't exactly woken up cheerful.

Her fingers closed over his as she reached for the coffee, and he felt that same wild need, that same jolt of electricity that shot through him every time she touched him. His hand tightened on the cup, and he slowly lifted his gaze to hers.

Her eyes were smoky, heavy with a passion he'd only dreamed about. Her cheeks were flushed, her lips moist and inviting. He knew they'd be warm and soft under his own.

There was no past at this moment, no future. Just a man and a woman where time had ceased to intrude.

"Annie."

His voice was no more than a ragged whisper, a plea. He set down the coffee cup and started to reach for her—

Someone knocked at the front door. Loudly.

"Jared! Wake up, you lazy bum. Your baby sister's here!"

He closed his eyes and swore heatedly. Of all the lousy timing! An expression of sheer panic flashed across Annie's face. She grabbed for the blanket in a knee-jerk reaction.

Jessica Stone burst through the front door, her arms filled with department-store bags. She stopped abruptly as she took in Annie and Jared.

"Oops." She started to turn, mumbling an apology, then quickly spun back around, her eyes widening. "Annie?" she whispered. "Annie Bailey?"

Annie couldn't help but smile at Jessica. They hadn't seen each other in almost four years, but Jared's sister looked the same, although maybe more beautiful. With her dark shining hair and blue eyes, she was a Stone sibling through and through.

What must she think! Annie thought as she bit back a groan. The last time Jessica had seen her, Annie was engaged to Jonathan. Now here she was, with Jared, after obviously spending the night in his trailer.

What else *could* she think?

Jared jumped up and stepped away, shoving his hands into his pockets. Good Lord, the way both she and Jared were acting, who wouldn't think something was going on?

With a laugh, Jessica dropped her bags, then bounced on the couch beside Annie and threw her arms around her. "Annie! Why didn't you tell me you were coming? When did you get here? How long are you staying?" Before she could even answer, Jessica hugged her again. "Oh, it's so good to see you!"

Warmed by Jessica's welcome but speechless, Annie sent an imploring look to Jared.

"Arloco Oil has agreed to back me," Jared said. "Annie is their geologist."

Jessica stared at Annie. "I'd almost forgotten. You *were* studying to be a geologist. Jonathan graduated a year before you."

Annie nodded.

Jessica shook her head in disbelief. "And now you're back here. Incredible."

"Incredible" didn't begin to describe it, Jared thought. "Why did you come back early? I thought you were in San Antonio with Jake and Savannah and Emma."

"We all got home last night, Jared. Like we were supposed to." Jessica frowned at him. "You never were very good at dates, big brother. I suppose you've also forgotten that Emma's tenth-birthday party is this afternoon, too."

"It is not." Jared grabbed the black T-shirt he'd set on the coffee table earlier and pulled it on. "It's next Saturday."

Jessica looked at Annie and sighed. "He's cute, but hopeless. I'll expect you both at the ranch this afternoon. Four o'clock."

"Oh, no." Annie shook her head. "I can't. I...well, I'm staying in town, and—"

"Great!" Jessica said brightly as she stood. "You can ride in from town with me then. We'll have lots of time to catch up."

Jessica gathered up the bags she'd dropped and deposited them in Jared's arms. "I know how much you love to shop," she said sarcastically, "so I picked up a few things for you in San Antonio. I'll send you the bill." She winked at him, then reached up and kissed his cheek. "Wear the shirt in the white bag this afternoon."

Jared frowned down at his sister. She had a mischievous look in her eyes, and he knew it meant trouble.

But there was no escaping whatever it was she was up to, he thought with a sigh. And so what if Annie was at the party? What harm was there in that? There'd be enough other people around to keep a safe distance from her, and it wasn't as if they were going home together.

He stared after his sister as she sashayed out the door with a wave, thinking there were tornadoes that caused less damage.

The last time Annie had been to Stone Creek Ranch there hadn't been pink balloons or streamers decorating the inside of the one-story brick house. There'd been no real laughter, as she heard now, no smiling faces. No brightly colored cake with huge pink roses. The people hadn't been dressed in party clothes. They'd worn black, and they'd come to say goodbye to friend and neighbor, Jonathan Stone.

For Annie, that day had been a blur. She'd sat with the family, talked with everyone there, but even now, she couldn't recall one conversation she'd had or the name of one person she'd met. All she remembered was the cocoon of pain, and the horrible overwhelming feeling that she'd forgotten something and couldn't remember what it was.

But today, when she'd stepped through the front door in a sheer floral-print dress, it was as if she'd moved from one time zone into another, from a dark place into a bright place, and though she'd felt a moment of panic, she also felt as if she belonged here. And when Jessica dragged her through all the other guests to Jake, the minute he wrapped his arms around her, whatever anxiety she'd been feeling was gone.

She felt as if she'd come home.

She hugged Jake back, then gasped when he lifted her off the floor, not a difficult feat for him, considering the fact that he was six foot four.

Jake set her down, then held her away from him and smiled the Stone smile that drove women crazy. "Annie Bailey. Tell me you're single, you gorgeous creature."

It was at that moment that Annie's gaze caught Jared's. He was leaning against the fireplace a few feet away, a bottle of beer in his hand, watching her intently. Black jeans hugged his narrow hips, and a deep blue Western-style shirt emphasized the blue of his eyes and dark hair. She felt her pulse race as he nodded at her, but made no move to join them.

Shaken, she turned her attention back to Jake and forced herself to grin at him. "I am single, but I hear you're not."

"Can't take my eyes off this man or he's into trouble." A slender blonde moved beside Jake and slid her arm through his. Her soft Southern accent was honey-smooth. "Watch out, Annie, or he'll break your heart like he did mine."

"I seem to recall it was the other way around," Jake said indignantly. "I'm the one who had to beg you to marry me in front of twenty little giggling girls."

"A fitting punishment for letting me get away in the first place," she reminded him coolly, but there was laughter and love in her eyes when she kissed him on the cheek. She turned back to Annie, her hand outstretched. "I'm Savannah."

Jessica, who had been standing beside Annie looking extremely amused, handed Annie a can of soda as she leaned close and whispered loudly, "I'll give you all the juicy details about these two later."

Jake frowned at Jessica, then looked at his wife. "What have you been telling her?"

Savannah smiled innocently. "Why, nothing, dear."

A little girl who was a young version of Jessica peeked curiously from behind Jake's back. Jake slipped an arm around the child and pulled her in front of him. "Annie, this is my sister, Emma. Emma, this is Annie Bailey, a good friend.''

Annie held out her hand. ''Happy birthday, Emma.''

Emma shyly took Annie's hand, then studied her for a long moment. ''You were in Jessica's movie.''

Annie furrowed her brow. ''Jessica's movie?''

Emma nodded. ''From her video camera. You were kissing my brother Jonathan, who went to heaven.''

Annie felt her throat thicken at Emma's innocent comment. Jessica had also been home from college the summer Annie had come to Stone Creek with Jonathan, and she'd brought a new video recorder with her. Every time Annie and Jonathan had turned around, Jessica was pointing the camera. Annie had forgotten all about that tape.

''Were you going to marry him?'' Emma asked.

There was an awkward moment, a hesitation in the space between heartbeats where Annie wasn't sure what to say. Savannah touched Emma's shoulder. ''Sweetheart, why don't we—''

''It's all right.'' Annie looked at Emma and smiled softly. ''Yes, honey, I was going to marry him.''

She glanced at Jared. His expression was blank, but still she noticed the subtle tightening of his shoulders and slight narrowing of his eyes, and she knew he'd heard their conversation.

''My mommy went to heaven, too,'' Emma said with understanding, then glanced up at Savannah. ''But I live with my Aunt Savannah and Jake now. They love me, too.''

It was easy to see the truth in Emma's statement as Jake and Savannah smiled down at the child. Through all the problems Annie knew they'd had, they were still a family.

A family who loved one another beyond anything else. A family that stayed together, no matter what.

Jonathan had wanted children, and so had she. He'd teased her that, because he was a twin, they'd have two sets in three years.

And now nearly four years had passed. Jonathan was gone, and there were no children. A dull ache settled in Annie's stomach.

She glanced at Jared again, and a sudden wave of uneasiness washed over her. Is that why she was so attracted to Jared? Was it possible that subconsciously she was trying to replace what she'd had with Jonathan? That on some level she'd realized how quickly time was moving on, realized that she might never have the family she so desperately wanted?

"Well, hello, again."

Annie turned at the sound of her name and nearly winced. It was Myrna. The circle of Stone siblings immediately tensed. Even Jared had pushed away from the fireplace and made his way toward them, a frown on his face.

"Mrs. Stone." Annie nodded at the woman.

Purple-and-green cloisonné earrings dangled from Myrna's ears, matching her green silk jumpsuit. "So lovely to see you again, dear."

Annie forced a smile, but did not respond. She felt torn between wishing she had an aspirin or a stiff drink, instead of the can of soda her fingers were tightly wrapped around.

Myrna gestured with her nearly empty wineglass. "So what does everyone think about Annie working for Jared?"

"Annie doesn't work for me." Jared moved beside Annie. "She already explained that to you."

"Well, not technically, but—"

"We think it's wonderful." A hard glint shone in Jake's eyes as he cut his stepmother off. "Why wouldn't we?"

"Annie is brilliant," Jessica chimed in. "Jared is lucky to have her working with him."

They were all protecting her, Annie realized. It didn't matter that all that time had passed. They still treated her now as they had then—as a member of the family. A warmth that even Myrna couldn't destroy spread through her.

"Well," Myrna said, lifting her chin, "I certainly never meant to imply that it wasn't a *good* thing. I just don't understand why Jared wants to risk everything for this project. Especially after I've offered him such a generous amount for the land. Daddy says—"

"What *do* I say, Myrna?"

Annie glanced at the silver-haired distinguished-looking man who had moved beside Myrna. His intense brown eyes settled on Annie and he smiled broadly.

"You must be Annie," he said and offered a hand. "I'm Myrna's father, Carlton Hewitt."

Annie took his hand. It was cool to the touch, and she felt a strength that surprised her for a man his age. "How do you do."

"I was just saying that Jared would be better off selling the land now," Myrna went on. "Everyone knows that oil drilling is risky. Hardly a sound investment."

"And I suppose that building a six-thousand-square-foot mansion in the middle of nowhere is your idea of a sound investment," Jared said tightly.

"It was, until J.T. left me with no land," she complained. "And if you—"

"Leave the boy be," Carlton said good-naturedly to his daughter. "A man has to do what he has to do. And Annie here must have thought the project a good one, or she wouldn't have allowed her company to back it. Would you, Annie?''

Annie felt an uneasiness as Carlton looked at her. ''It's a viable project, Mr. Hewitt. The figures are extremely promising.''

Carlton smiled. ''Well, then, Jared, all my best to you. And as much as my daughter wants this, I'm afraid she'll just have to find herself land somewhere else.''

''I don't want land somewhere else.'' Myrna pouted. ''I have a beautiful home I love and I have no intention of leaving. Jake and Jared won't even part with a few hundred acres. Not to mention Jessica. I've offered her a fair sum for her parcel, and she insists on converting that old town into a children's camp, for heaven's sake. It's simply not safe for a young woman to move out there by herself with all those construction workers.''

Two sets of deep blue male eyes turned toward Jessica.

''What's she talking about?'' both Jake and Jared said at the same time.

Savannah took Emma's hand. ''Time to go check on the ice cream,'' she said, slipping away.

Jessica's eyes narrowed with irritation as she stared at Myrna. ''And how did you come across that information?''

''Your landlady, Mrs. Wimple, told me that you'd given one months' notice, and Mr. Barret at the building department mentioned you'd applied for a permit. Oh, dear.'' Myrna's expression of concern was almost comical. ''Was this a secret, dear?''

''God forbid there'd be a secret in this town,'' Jessica muttered, then turned to smile weakly at her brothers. They scowled fiercely. ''I was going to tell you,'' she insisted.

Annie watched as the three of them began to argue in earnest over Jessica going out to her ghost town by herself. Myrna had certainly done it again, Annie thought with disgust.

When someone yelled that there was a phone call for Jessica, she mumbled something about being saved by the bell and quickly disappeared. Carlton slipped an arm around his daughter and suggested they both freshen their drinks before Myrna could start in again.

"Jessie's not going out there by herself," Jake said flatly when Myrna and her father were gone.

"No way in hell," Jared agreed.

Annie smiled to herself. Something told her that no matter how determined the two men were, Jessica was equally determined. It would be interesting to see who won, she thought with amusement.

Except I won't be here to see it, she reminded herself, and she felt a heaviness in her chest so profound she had to take a few deep breaths.

Jake was pulled away then by three little girls begging to start the piñata. She and Jared were left alone. They stood there for a long moment, both of them glancing around the room, feeling strangely awkward. She took a sip of her soda, but the liquid felt dry as it slid down her throat.

A man bumped her from behind, and she turned as he apologized. When she turned back, she caught Jared's gaze skimming over her. Her pulse skipped at the look of pure male hunger she saw in his eyes. He looked quickly away.

Dammit, Jared, don't look at me like that, then turn away!

She heard a loud whack, then the shrieks of little girls. She wondered if they'd accept a live male, instead of a piñata.

"Did you get Slater settled in town?" she asked, groping for conversation.

Yeah, Jared thought irritably. *And he talked about you all night.* Jared had already decided he was going to have to keep a close eye on his foreman and Miss Annie Bailey. Not that he didn't trust Slater completely, he just thought it would be a good idea if the man didn't get sidetracked.

And now, as he looked at Annie, he realized *he* was the one getting sidetracked. The dress she had on was pure femininity: long and swirling around her shapely legs, quite sheer but concealing enough to hide what was necessary. She'd tucked the sides of her hair up with gold clips, and the glossy rose-colored lipstick she wore kept whispering at him to stare at her mouth.

"What about you?" he said, tearing his gaze away from her. "How're you doing with the map?"

"It's coming along. I just need a little more time."

They lapsed into a strained silence again. Annie cleared her throat, and he could tell her smile was forced. "I think I'll go see if Savannah can use some help."

He took hold of her arm as she started to turn away. They both felt the jolt and their eyes met. "Annie, I... You look—"

"Jared!" someone yelled from across the room. "Jessica says she needs to talk to you pronto in Jake's office."

At that second, Jared wasn't sure whether to thank his sister or throttle her. He'd almost told Annie how beautiful she was. How glad he was she was here. This was the second time Jessica had "saved" him from stepping over the line he'd drawn when it came to Annie.

That was what he wanted, wasn't it? To keep his distance from her? And even if it wasn't what he wanted, it was the way it had to be.

He dropped his hand from Annie's arm and his fingers felt cold and empty. Hell, *he* felt cold and empty.

Whatever it was that his sister wanted, it had better be good.

He moved away from Annie, felt her gaze follow him as he left the room. He was silently cursing when he walked into the office.

Jessica was on the phone, raking her fingers through her hair as she spoke. "I'm on my way, Mrs. James. Yes, I'll find him, don't worry. I'll see you in thirty minutes."

Jared frowned as he closed the door behind him. "What's the matter?"

"Jared, I'm sorry, but one of my kids from the youth group has run away. I'm sure he'll show up, but I've got to get over to his house and calm his mother down." She grabbed her purse and dug for her keys. "I don't know when I'll be back, so you're going to have to take Annie home for me."

"But—"

She kissed him on the cheek and was out the door. "Thanks, big brother, I knew you wouldn't mind," she called over her shoulder.

He stood there, struck by the force of his tornado sister and stared at the open door. *Oh, no.* He closed his eyes and swore softly. It was a long drive into town. Forty-five minutes long.

Dammit, dammit, dammit.

He took a deep breath and walked back out to the party. Annie was standing in a corner, talking to Sam McCants, who owned the ranch next to Jake's. Jared remembered Jake's being crazy with jealousy when Sam had turned his attention on Savannah. Now, Jared realized as he watched Annie laugh at something Sam said, it was *his* turn to feel crazy.

And he also realized that forty-five minutes with Annie, alone, late at night, was forty-four minutes and thirty seconds longer than he could handle without making him want things he couldn't have.

They drove to town with the truck windows rolled down. It was warm, and the air, heavy with the scent of sage, rippled through the cab. The headlights lit the dark deserted highway, but the moon was so bright that lights were hardly necessary.

"Jared, really, you didn't need to drive me back to town," Annie protested for the third time since they'd left the party. "There must have been someone else headed in my direction."

"I told you it's no problem," Jared said flatly. If he'd been left alone to consume the amount of liquor he'd wanted to it might have been a problem, but Jake had dragged him off to help with games before he'd even had a chance to finish one beer.

He flipped on the radio, and a country ballad about a lonely bedroom and empty pillows filled the cab. He quickly snapped the radio off again.

With a sigh, Annie leaned her head back against the seat and stared out the windshield. The silence stretched as long as the highway, and when she closed her eyes, Jared thought she might have fallen asleep.

He glanced at her, at the slender column of her neck and the smooth line of her jaw. A longing he couldn't suppress gripped his insides. *If only...*

"Your sister-in-law is terrific," Annie said, interrupting his thoughts. "Jonathan told me once what Jake's ex-wife put him through. I'm glad to see him so happy."

It had been a rough time for Jake, Jared remembered. He and Jessica had felt so helpless.

"We thought he'd never settle down again," Jared said. "It took a special lady like Savannah to set him straight."

There was a long quiet pause. Annie turned slowly and opened her eyes.

"And what about you, Jared?" she said softly. "What kind of special woman is it going to take to set you straight?"

The cab suddenly felt like a fist closing around him. How the hell was he supposed to answer that?

The lights of town were quickly approaching. A few more minutes. That was all he needed to hold it together.

"I didn't know I needed straightening out," he said lightly, trying to force a humor into his voice he certainly didn't feel.

He smiled at her, but she didn't smile back. She simply stared at him, not even bothering to brush away the strands of hair whispering over her face.

He pulled into the parking lot of the motel and cut the engine. He stared straight ahead, his hands still on the wheel.

"It's Jonathan, isn't it?" she said quietly. "He's the reason you haven't married. Why you aren't with someone. Because you won't allow yourself that happiness, will you?"

His fingers tightened on the steering wheel.

"Or is it just me?" Her voice was barely a whisper. "Do you look at me and think of Jonathan? Do you wish I would just go away so you wouldn't have to be reminded of him?"

When he didn't answer, she turned away and started to open the door. He reached out and took hold of her arm, then gently pulled her across the seat beside him. He looked down at her, and the moisture in her eyes only deepened the ache in his chest.

"I do think of Jonathan every time I look at you," he said raggedly. "He's the one who deserves to be looking at you, to be touching you." He closed his eyes and swallowed the bitter taste in his throat. "He's the one you should be with, Annie. Not me. Never me."

She touched his cheek with her fingers, and he sucked in a deep breath at the gentle touch. "Jonathan is gone, Jared. Nothing can bring him back."

He opened his eyes and watched as a tear slid down her cheek. "But you're here." She lifted her face to his. "And so am I."

His heart went still, then pounded so hard he thought his chest might explode. His fingers tightened on her arm.

I have to taste her. If only this one time... just one time....

He lowered his mouth to hers.

She met him, softly at first, and her sigh was like warm silk sliding over his jaw. It was the merest brush of lips, no more than a whisper, but it set his blood pounding in his veins. Sensation after sensation pulsed through him. Every nerve ending in his body became excruciatingly alive.

She opened to him, and the sweetness he found there made it impossible not to want more. He moaned deeply, a desperate mixture of need and despair. She pressed against him, sliding her fingers up his chest, burning his skin through the fabric of his shirt.

An urgency coursed through him, and he pulled her closer, slanting his mouth fiercely against hers again and again. She met the hot thrust of his tongue with her own and the whimper of need in her throat sent him over the edge.

Every primal instinct screamed at him that she was *his*. She belonged to him. He buried his hands in her hair, pulling her closer. She welcomed him, accepted him fully, and when his hand closed over her breast, she cried out, arching into him. His thumb slid over her hardened nipple, and she moved against him, gasping for breath.

He needed as he'd never needed before. Ached as he'd never ached before. His body demanded fulfillment, and he bent her backward onto the seat of the truck, covering her body with his, moving against her, spreading her thighs with his knee . . .

What the hell was he thinking?

Appalled at what he'd done, what he was about to do, he sat up quickly, pulling her up with him.

"Annie, my God . . ."

He sucked in a breath and dropped his hands from her. His body was on fire, his arousal to the point of pain. "Annie, I'm sorry."

She stared at him, her passion-filled eyes wide with confusion. Slowly she eased away from him and combed her hair away from her face with her fingers. The look in her eyes was like a knife ripping him in two.

"I'm sorry, too, Jared." She opened the door and slipped out, then stood outside the truck and leveled her gaze with his.

"You feel guilty because every time you look at me you see Jonathan's face," she said heavily. "But you know why I feel guilty, Jared?"

She closed the door and stared at him through the open window. Her voice was so quiet he could barely hear her.

"Because every time you look at me," she said, her voice shaking, "every time you touch me, I can't even remember what Jonathan looked like."

She turned and walked away. He wanted to call out to her, to jump out of the truck and bring her back to him. To hold her in his arms and tell her it was all right.

But it wasn't all right. And it never would be.

So he watched her go.

Six

The smell of damp earth filled the air as Annie watched the first-shift crew awaken the long-sleeping derrick. There was an energy here she'd never experienced before. A powerful force that charged the air and ground. It made her skin tingle and her pulse quicken.

Of course, for Annie there was always a certain level of excitement the first day of drilling. She compared it to the first day of school after the summer break, when everything was new and you were unsure of what to expect, unsure if you were going to like your teachers, of who would be in your classes. Then as the semester wore on, the days would settle into a routine, then finally boredom. She'd learned quickly that drilling a rig was no different.

Until this rig.

Jared stood beside her, hands on his hips, watching mud bubble up from the entry hole. All the drilling fluid would be routed into a mud pit, which was a hole in the ground the size of a house. It was also from where she would be retrieving her soil samples as they moved closer to the target zone.

"What's your estimated time to set the casing?" Annie yelled over the roar of the machinery.

"Around three this afternoon," he shouted over his shoulder, then signaled for the man leading the drill to slow the speed.

"Are you going to watch?" she asked.

He nodded. "I want to make sure everything goes smoothly."

She knew he would, of course. Until everything was in place and he could see how the crews were working together, Annie had expected Jared to do double shifts. Besides, it was much easier to avoid her that way.

When she'd shown up this morning, he'd acted as if nothing at all had happened between them after Emma's party. He'd been business as usual.

He was one stubborn man, she thought dryly.

But no matter how he acted, no matter how hard he pretended, the undeniable draw was still there between them. Lord knew *she* was still reeling from that kiss. And no amount of pretending could make it go away.

Jared called out to Slater, who was busy checking the compressor gauges. The foreman gave Jared an okay sign, then pointed at Annie and gave her a wink. Annie smiled back and waved. Jared frowned.

A woman on a rig was still a novelty for most crews, and not everyone was completely accepting. She could usually tell immediately which men were going to give her trouble, and she dealt with them accordingly. But the members of this crew had greeted her without a hint of resentment, and she wondered if she had Slater to thank for that, or Jared.

She'd also noticed that Glenn Woods and Steve Mc-Bain, two of the new recruits Slater had rounded up, had been watching her with puppy-dog eyes, but she'd dealt with that type of infatuation before, and it didn't bother her. As long as they did their work, Annie didn't mind the covert glances and repeated excuses to talk with her.

They would drill to twelve thousand feet, which would take approximately three weeks. If there was no oil found once the designated target was hit, work was to stop and the rig was to shut down. Arloco would cease to pay any bills submitted beyond that point. There was no such thing as bad weather, days off or holidays.

The clock was ticking.

At three-thirty that afternoon, Slater, Jared and Annie opened a bottle of champagne and a bag of pretzels in the office. It was the end of the first day's shift, everything had gone smoothly, and the casing was in place. They were all tired but smiling as the glasses were raised.

"Here's to all that money you're gonna make," Slater said, clinking Jared's glass with his own. "May you remember all of us little people as you sail off in your yacht."

"I might remember a lot of things," Jared said, taking a sip of wine and reaching for a pretzel, "but not one of them will be you as one of the little people."

Slater's booming laugh shook the trailer walls and Annie laughed with him. Jared watched her eyes light up, and when her lips touched the champagne glass in her hand, he desperately wanted to taste her while the bubbles still lingered in her mouth.

He cursed himself for the thousandth time for wanting her as he did. He'd finally given up denying it. After that kiss the other night, he'd be a bigger fool than he already was if he didn't at least admit to himself he was attracted to Annie.

But it was more than an attraction. It went deeper than that, more intense. She'd aroused more than his body; she'd aroused his very soul, made him want her in a way he could never have her.

"Hey, boss, you look like something the cat dragged in." Slater refilled his now empty glass, then topped off Annie's again. "Don't you think so, Bailey?"

Annie looked at Jared and nodded. "Yeah, after the dog finished with it."

Outwardly Jared frowned at their antics, but the impish light in Annie's hazel eyes made him smile inside. Her face was smudged with dirt, her hair tousled, and her jeans and boots covered with mud.

She looked beautiful.

It was all he could do not to pull her onto his lap and cover that smudged face with kisses.

"Well, Slater," Jared drawled, stretching his long legs out in front of him, "in case you hadn't noticed, you're wearing enough mud to build a dam. I'd get you a mirror, but the way you look, you'd just break it."

Slater feigned indignation and Annie giggled. Jared grinned at her. "And you, Miss Angel Face, the way your mug looks right now, you could be the poster child for the homeless."

Annie threw the first pretzel, but from there it was hard to keep an account. Pretzels and champagne flew, and they were all laughing so hard they didn't even hear the knock or the office door open.

"Uh, excuse me."

Jared ducked a salty missile Annie had aimed at his head, then turned at the sound of the man's voice.

He wasn't one of the crew. In fact, Jared had never seen him before. He was young, around twenty-five, with red hair and pale freckled skin. He was carrying a clipboard and a small black book.

The man picked his way through the broken pretzels and puddles of champagne covering the office floor, then reached into the pocket of his blue plaid shirt and pulled out a card.

"Boyd Fitzer," the man said loudly, as if he were announcing royalty. "Department of Oil and Gas."

Jared rose from his chair and took the business card. "What can I do for you, Mr. Fitzer?"

"I need to see your drilling permits."

Jared frowned. "I've filed all the necessary paperwork and been approved. I've also been told twice on the phone that everything is in order."

"Well, then—" Fitzer raised one red eyebrow "—you should have your permits, shouldn't you?"

Jared felt a muscle in his cheek jump. "Your department has been a little slow mailing them out."

The man raised his other eyebrow. "So you started drilling without them?"

At the murderous look on Jared's face, Annie felt it best to intercede. "Mr. Fitzer," she asked sweetly, "how long have you worked for the department?"

He straightened his shoulders. "Three months."

Annie groaned silently. The most difficult department employees were always the new ones.

She smiled brightly at the man. "Well, then, perhaps you aren't aware that it's not unusual for a rig to start without the permit in hand once there's verbal approval. You know how slow the postal service can be."

He hesitated, then shook his head and tapped the small black book he carried. "I'm afraid that's not in the code book. And besides," he added, "I have no record of your paperwork."

"No record!" Jared slammed his hands down on the desk. The glasses rattled. "What the hell are you talking about?"

At Jared's outburst, Fitzer dropped his clipboard and book. "There, uh, there's no paperwork. I looked for it personally when I was assigned to you."

Jared's stream of expletives singed the air. His face red, Fitzer bent to pick up his clipboard, but Slater, who had been sitting back quietly, reached for it first and handed it to the man. Slater then reached for the code book and began to leaf casually through it.

Flustered, the state employee ran a hand through his hair. "Mr. Stone, I'm sorry, but I'm afraid I'm going to have to shut you down until you have the proper permits."

Now you've done it, Fitzer, Annie thought, shaking her head. This boy really had a lot to learn about oilmen.

"Shut us down!" Jared came around the desk, his fists clenched. "You think you can—"

"Here it is, Jared," Slater interjected, stabbing a finger at the code book. "Remember that code we were talking about the other day?"

"What code?" Jared yelled.

"You know, the one where it says it's legal to shoot stupid civil servants."

Slater stood and looked down at Fitzer. The poor man's Adam's apple bobbed as he looked up at his huge adversary.

"You . . . you c-can't threaten me," Fitzer said weakly.

"I remember now," Jared said, his eyes narrowing as he turned his gaze on the younger man, "but wasn't it just stupid civil servants with red hair?"

"Yep." Slater slammed the book and tossed it at Fitzer. "That's the one."

Fitzer caught the book and stumbled backward. "You're shut down, Mr. Stone," he said, his voice wavering. "As of now."

When Jared made a move toward Fitzer, he turned and ran, slipping once in a puddle of champagne before disappearing out the door.

"He could have at least closed the door behind him," Slater muttered. "Guy must have been raised in a barn."

For the next three days, Jared paced like a caged animal. The wait was driving him insane. Hell, he was past the point of insanity, he thought, dragging both hands through his hair, then over his unshaved face. He'd shifted into lunatic sometime yesterday afternoon. Right after Annie's phone call telling him there was nothing to tell him.

She'd driven to Midland two days ago to handle the problem in person. Jared had wanted to go himself, but she and Slater had convinced him that the rage he was in would only make matters worse. Slater had also threatened to lock him in the toolshed if he tried to go anywhere, and from the determined look on the big man's face, Jared knew he wasn't bluffing.

Reluctantly Jared had agreed, but now, as he stared out his front window watching the dark clouds move in quickly over the horizon, he wished he hadn't. His insides were wound up tighter than a spring fitting, and if he didn't do something soon, he was going to explode.

The only bright spot at this point was that they still had their crew. Slater had managed to convince the men to hang in there a few days. Now all the foreman had to do was keep an eye on everyone to make sure that restless men with too much time on their hands didn't get into too much trouble or hit the bars to excess. Glenn and Tom had asked Jared to join them in a few games of poker, but he wouldn't have had the concentration to play a game of go fish.

Clenching his fists, he stared at the bottle of whiskey on the counter, then continued his pacing. He almost wished he smoked. He may have had a lot of bad habits, but that was one he'd never picked up. He stared at the bottle on the counter again, then swore and kicked a pillow he'd thrown earlier, pretending it was that weasel Fitzer's head.

What the hell was taking so long? It was after seven; the permit department had been closed for two hours. Why hadn't she called?

He needed to hear her voice. Even if it was no news. Even if it was *bad* news. He just wanted to hear that soft sexy voice of hers and know that she was all right. That she would be coming back soon.

He paused at the flash of lightning. The rain started off as a murmur and quickly escalated to a shout, pounding the trailer roof with brutal force. Thunder shook the walls.

He felt trapped. He had to do something. Anything.

He reached for the bottle.

It was after eight by the time Annie pulled in front of Jared's trailer. The rain had settled into a heavy consistent staccato, and an occasional streak of lightning illuminated the dark sky. She started to get out of her car, then realized it was dark inside the trailer and Jared's truck was gone. Disappointment was like a dull knife in her chest. She'd driven straight here from Midland, not even bothering to stop in town first.

Where was he? In town maybe, but she doubted that. He'd been staying close to the rig since the disaster with Fitzer. She'd been able to reach him here or at the rig.

Which left the rig. But what would he be doing there at this hour? And in this rain?

With a weary sigh, she turned her car around and headed for the oil well. She was tired and hungry and desperately wanted a hot shower. But first she had to see Jared. It couldn't wait.

As she neared the office, she could see a light on in the trailer. So he *was* working. She shook her head, wondering why that should surprise her.

She'd missed him. She'd told herself she was an idiot, but it didn't make any difference. Every time she'd called him, just before they'd hang up, she'd have the crazy urge to tell him, but she didn't. She couldn't.

He was in there now. She could picture him sitting at the desk, his dark hair rumpled, his brow furrowed, his deep blue eyes intense as he studied a chart or a log. She smiled at the image, and her pulse jumped at the thought of seeing him.

She cut the engine of her car and stepped out, preparing to make a mad dash to the office. Thunder rattled the heavens and lightning struck no more than fifty yards away from the rig, illuminating the entire area.

Startled, Annie turned. The derrick glowed from the flash of light and on the platform was the silhouette of a man dressed in black, his coat billowing behind him like the wings of a raven, his arms outstretched.

She froze, staring up at the apparition.

It can't be, it can't be . . .

She'd seen this in her nightmares—Jonathan up on the platform of the rig, his gaze locked with hers as he stepped to the edge. She'd open her mouth to scream, but no sound would come out. . . .

She tried to scream now, but it was the same as her dream—no sound came out. She squeezed her eyes shut and fell to her knees in the mud. *It wasn't him. It wasn't possible....*

Rain soaked her clothes and hair. She opened her eyes again, but all she saw was blackness now.

"Annie!"

When someone grabbed her arms and pulled her up, she did scream.

"Annie, it's me, Jared."

"Jared?" she said weakly, then swayed. He tightened his hold on her and hauled her into his arms. She started to shake.

"Jared, I thought you were... I thought that..." She wrapped her arms around him.

"I know," he said against her ear. "I know. I'm sorry."

He pulled her into her car and climbed in beside her. They were both soaking wet. Neither one of them spoke while he drove them back to his place. The rain and her teeth chattering were the only sounds.

"Do you have any clothes in the car?" he asked as he pulled in front of the trailer.

She nodded. "My bag is in the back seat."

He reached around and grabbed it, then took her hand and led her inside. "Go ahead and get in the shower. I'll make us some coffee."

She started to protest, but Jared took her face in his hands and forced her to look at him. Her face was pale, so pale it frightened him. "Do what I say, Annie Bailey, or I'll drag you in there myself."

She smiled at him and a touch of color came back to her cheeks. Without thinking, he kissed the end of her wet nose, then released her.

When she came out a few minutes later, dressed in a pink blouse and jeans, he sat her on the couch, shoved a cup of coffee into her hands, then took a quick shower himself.

By the time he came out, the color had returned completely to her face, and she was working on a second cup of coffee. Her damp hair curled around her cheeks.

He poured himself a cup and sat on the couch beside her.

They sat there for a long moment, listening to the rain.

"You okay now?" he finally asked.

She nodded. "Yes, I..." She turned her head away. "Oh, Jared, I feel like an idiot."

"Don't." He touched her shoulder. She'd stopped shaking, and he could feel the warmth of her skin through the cotton blouse she wore. "It was stupid of me to try and catch your attention like that."

"What were you doing up there?"

"It was either sit around my place and get drunk or come down here and work. I was headed for the office when I noticed a pulley was loose. I'm sorry I scared you."

She held her coffee cup in both hands. Steam rose from the black liquid and she stared at it. "It was raining that night, wasn't it?" she asked quietly.

His hand tightened on her shoulder. "Don't do this, Annie."

She shook her head. "No. It's all right." She looked up at him. "Jared, not talking about it doesn't mean it never happened. It did happen. There's nothing anyone can do to change that."

He held her soft gaze, then released a slow breath. "Yes, it was raining."

"Do you know what happened, I mean, what really happened?"

I lost my brother. My best friend. The only person who ever really knew me. The ache in his chest swelled until Jared thought he might not be able to breathe.

"There—" he swallowed back the thickness in his throat "—there was a cable loose. I told him to wait.... We'd get it in the morning when we could see better and the rain stopped. He...he was anxious and went, anyway."

Jared could hear the thunder, see the flash of lightning. But it was another storm, another time, not the one he'd just come out of.

"Slater and I followed Jonathan up the platform," he said as if he were narrating a film moving through his head, "giving him a bad time about being green. He just laughed and said the only thing green about him was all the money he was going to make."

Annie watched as Jared stared, unblinking, at the coffee in his hands. There was no emotion on his face. No expression.

But his eyes. God, his eyes. The torment she saw there ripped through her like a sword. Pain welled up inside her, and her own eyes filled with tears. She set down her coffee, then took Jared's cup out of his hands. His fingers were stiff and cold.

"I was still several feet away," Jared went on, his voice empty, "when he reached for the cable and slipped. I...I couldn't stop him. I couldn't help him...."

He stared at her then, his eyes wide, and grabbed her by the shoulders. "A few feet. A few lousy miserable feet."

She touched his face. He'd shaved after his shower and his skin was smooth under her fingertips. "I loved him, too," she said softly.

He made a wild choking sound in his throat and closed his eyes. There was nothing she could say. There were no words. She'd dealt with her grief long ago, but Jared hadn't. He needed this, and there was no easy way.

Letting her heart lead her, she touched her lips lightly to his, then slid her arms around his waist and pressed her

cheek against his chest. His arms were wooden as they
came around her, but slowly, as they sat there, he began to
relax. She listened to the steady thud of his heart.

And then she remembered.

She straightened. "Jared, I almost forgot. We got the
permit. We're back in business."

He stared at her blankly, as if he'd forgotten. Then he
smiled slowly and pulled her close. She wrapped her arms
around his neck and smiled back. His hands were warm
now as they circled her waist, and she was suddenly aware
of the hard length of his body against hers. His heart began to pound harder, and she knew that he was every bit
as aware of her as she was of him.

She started to move away, knowing that the second he
realized what they were feeling he would push her away,
but his arms tightened, holding her in place.

She was afraid to look at him, terrified of what she
would see. Pity? Or another explanation of why he
couldn't let himself touch her, or want her.

But when she lifted her gaze to his, what she saw there—
the raw open need, the steel blue intensity in his eyes—
made her heart stop.

He touched her face with his fingertips, as if he was really touching her, really seeing her, for the first time.

"Annie," he said raggedly, then covered her mouth with
his.

Seven

It was madness. He knew that, but it made no difference. He was beyond thinking, beyond reason. The price he'd pay would be high, but even that realization couldn't stop him.

He pulled her closer, needing to feel her body against his. She was soft and warm in his arms, her lips incredibly sweet. Desire, stronger than he'd ever felt, hotter than he'd ever imagined, pounded in his veins and through his body.

He'd meant to be gentle. He wanted to be, but his control shattered when she parted her lips and welcomed him. All the wanting and the needing washed over him, and he tightened his hold, grinding his mouth against hers again and again, murmuring her name.

Her arms circled his shoulders and a small sound of need in Annie's throat sent his senses spinning. She was so small against him, so soft and vulnerable. He wanted her so badly he worried he might hurt her. The thought terrified him and he started to pull away, but she clung to him, deepening the kiss as she tugged him closer, meeting every thrust of his tongue with her own.

He was lost to her, and yet, at the same time, it was as if he was found. As if, for the first time in his life, he was where he belonged.

She tasted like an exotic wine, so rich that one sip made him drunk, so rare that he knew he'd never find it again. The moan that came from deep in his throat was not one of desire, but of torment, knowing that this could never be enough, but that it would have to be.

Her hands began to move over him, and he ceased to think at all. He allowed himself to feel, to cherish every touch, every taste, every sound. She *was* his. If only for this moment, she was.

Annie could hardly breathe. No man had ever made her feel this way before. She felt a desperation that shocked her, a need to consume and be consumed she'd never experienced. A need she was sure could never be fulfilled, but still insisted—no, *demanded*—fulfillment nonetheless. She felt the energy coiled inside Jared, felt his muscles tighten and bunch as she moved her hands down his arms and over his chest. The strength she knew he possessed excited her all the more. She squirmed against him, thinking she would never be close enough.

In one fluid movement he pulled her beneath him, and she sank into the soft cushions of the couch, his body stretched over hers. He dragged his hot lips over her cheek and jaw, then down her neck, setting her skin on fire. He moved lower, cupping her breasts in his hands, sliding his mouth over the fullness, kissing her through the cloth separating them.

With a gasp, she buried her fingers in his damp hair, frustrated at the barriers between them. Gently he bit through the fabric of her blouse, closing his mouth over her nipple and sucking. Pain and pleasure rocketed through her, and she arched upward, catching her lower lip between her teeth as she cried out.

"Jared," she said hoarsely, "please...please..."

Her plea was like lighter fluid on an already burning fire. Jared pulled her blouse upward, baring her stomach. He thought of hot satin as he moved downward over the smooth white valley. Her fingers moved over his head and through his hair as he nuzzled her small perfect belly button, dipping his tongue in and out so he might taste her there.

Annie caught her breath at the exquisite sensation of pleasure pulsating through her. Her hands clutched at him, tightening into fists. She couldn't bear it. She couldn't. He unsnapped the top button of her jeans, then shifted his attention upward again. He pushed her blouse higher, sliding his hands underneath to cup her breasts again. His lips moved over the thin silk covering her nipples, and she squirmed, desperately wanting to be free of the constraints of clothing.

"Annie," he whispered, his voice ragged and strained, "you're so sweet, so incredibly sweet."

He reached behind her and she arched upward as he unsnapped her bra and pushed it away. He met the welcoming tip of her nipple with his tongue, and when he closed his mouth over the hardened peak he felt her entire body tense, heard her sharp intake of breath. He moved over her, giving equal attention to the soft mounds he'd cupped in his hands, reveling in the pleasure he gave her.

Her pleasure heightened his own, and an urgency began to fill him. He moved downward again, with his mouth and his hands, finding her zipper and tugging it down. The soft rasp mingled with the sound of the rain and their breathing. He wanted to taste her, to know every inch of her, and his lips followed as he slid the jeans down her hips and thighs, pulling her underwear with them. She surged upward as his lips moved over her, and he whispered to her, calming her, wanting so desperately to love her.

Annie's world was out of control. She was spinning somewhere, lost, in a place where pain and pleasure were one. Jared's hands slid over her hips and the texture of his rough palms on her skin sent shivers coursing through her. His fingers skimmed over her inner thighs and she dug her hands into his shoulders, twisting the fabric of his T-shirt in her fists. He made love to her as no man ever had before, stroking and touching, moving over her with a rhythm so profound she thought she might scream.

"Jared...please...I want you." She knew she was begging now. She didn't care.

He stood and pulled off his T-shirt. She watched him undress, and his dark heated gaze never left her as he stepped out of his jeans and underwear and tossed them aside.

Her heart slammed in her chest as he stared down at her. He was a beautiful man, solid muscle and long lean limbs. His arousal should have frightened her, but it only increased her desire. She reached out to him and he took her hand, moving over her as he kissed each finger and ran his tongue along the inside of her palm. She trembled, sure that if he didn't hurry she was going to die.

His lips moved over her body again, over her shoulder and sensuously over her breasts as he removed the last of her clothing. She slid her hands over his chest and hips. He sucked in a breath when she touched his inner thigh, then moaned when her fingers circled him. He was velvet over steel, and the raw power held her in awe.

He moved between her knees and spread her legs to make room for him. The storm outside increased; lightning and thunder shook the walls, rain pounded the roof. Neither one of them noticed or cared. The storm inside was the only one to be reckoned with, the only one that mattered.

"Look at me, Annie," he said, his voice heavy. "You have to look at me."

Through a mist of passion she lifted her gaze to his. His eyes were dark and fierce, piercing, and she couldn't have looked away if she'd wanted to. Her hands gripped the cushions beneath her and she curled her fingers tightly around the soft fabric. A flash of lightning illuminated the room, bathing their bodies in silver.

Jared entered her slowly as lightning flashed again, and he felt as if he were being torn from the darkness into a brilliant light. He had never known such intense pleasure, would never have even thought it possible. Her body was a tight velvet glove, and she wrapped her long sleek legs around him, drawing him closer. She arched upward, bringing them closer still, brushing her hardened nipples against his chest.

He began to move, slowly at first, nearly withdrawing, then easing himself in again. Annie clutched his arms, calling his name as she lifted her hips.

"Jared . . . Jared . . . please . . . hurry . . ."

His name on her lips was all he needed to lose the last thread of control. He took hold of her hips and buried himself deeply in her, moving with an urgency that had built to a fever pitch. Sweat beaded his brow, and they set a rhythm as wild as the beating of their hearts and as old as time.

Annie felt the tension build in her, higher and tighter, hotter, until it became so unbearable she began to shudder. She cried out as the first wave exploded through her, opening her eyes wide with a sharp gasp as the second one followed in its wake. She sobbed his name, digging her nails into his arms. His muscles flexed and he thrust wildly, until his own climax ripped through him.

It was impossible to say how much time passed. Their breathing had long since slowed, and the fine sheen of sweat on their bodies had cooled. Even the storm outside had calmed. Still locked in each other's arms, they listened to the soft rhythm of the rain.

Annie ran her fingers idly through Jared's dark hair. She didn't think herself capable of lifting more than her hand at the moment. She felt as if she were drifting like a child's balloon carried slowly on the breeze. When she sighed, he turned his head and kissed her neck.

"I'm too heavy," he said, and started to move away.

"No." She pulled him back. "You're perfect."

Rising up on his elbows, he stared down at her and smiled. "I was thinking the same thing about you."

She smiled back, wondering why she'd never noticed the small scar under his right eyebrow or the slight bump at the bridge of his nose. She rose upward and kissed both spots, then lightly brushed her lips across his.

"I wonder if we're both thinking the same thing now," she whispered.

He laughed softly, and the response from his body was her answer. She wrapped her arms around his neck, dragging his mouth to hers. His kiss was long and hot, seductive, and the flame ignited once again.

No woman had ever made him burn like this, Jared realized through the haze of pleasure. No woman had ever made him want more than he could have.

Why does it have to be Annie? he thought with despair. *It can't be Annie.*

But it was, and the time was past changing that fact. He refused to allow himself to think about tomorrow. It was difficult to think at all with Annie's hands skimming over his body like a silk scarf.

He raised himself over her, watching her face as he slid into her again. She held his gaze, her eyes deep pools of desire, her lips parted softly. As he moved deeper she gasped and arched her back. Her skin was flushed, her nipples hard.

And when her soft cries turned frantic and his own control shattered, the madness overtook them again.

The sun hadn't fully appeared over the distant mountains when Annie awoke the next morning. The rain had stopped and outside the open bedroom window, a blue jay squawked an irritable greeting. A soft breeze filtered through the wooden window blinds, carrying the scent of rain-dampened earth and fresh air.

She lay on her side, her back pressed against Jared's chest. The heat radiating off his body was like a furnace, and there had been no need for covers. In fact, the covers seemed to have disappeared off the bed completely, though she couldn't quite recall when that had happened.

Remembering her lack of inhibition with Jared, she felt her cheeks flush. They'd gone to bed, but hadn't fallen asleep until the wee hours of the morning, and even then the spirit had certainly been willing, though their bodies had not.

He slept peacefully now, with one arm looped tightly over her waist, and she turned carefully so she could face him. He breathed deeply, and she watched the rise and fall of his broad chest with open admiration. She smiled, noting his chest was only one of several attributes she admired.

Annie rose slowly, not wanting to wake him. She needed a few minutes alone before she faced him. She was too vulnerable right now, and she wanted to fortify her defenses. As she slipped quietly from under his arm, he stirred and his brow furrowed, but he didn't wake.

A chambray shirt hung over a chair beside the night-stand and she reached for it and tugged it on. Glancing back at him before she left the room, she found it took every ounce of willpower not to climb back into bed and wake him the way she truly wanted to. With her lips and her hands. With the words that she'd somehow managed not to speak last night.

I love you, Jared Stone.

They were dangerous words right now. She knew he wouldn't believe her. Lord knew, she could hardly believe it herself. But Jared was filled with too much guilt. He wasn't ready to allow himself the happiness she knew he deserved.

Last night there'd been a crack in that facade he'd built. But today she knew he'd rebuild it. She shook her head and silently left the bedroom. The man was too damn stubborn for his own good.

Jared awoke slowly. His arms felt heavy, his legs incapable of movement. A profound and complete satisfaction settled through his body. He'd either died or been drugged.

He moved a finger, then a toe. He was alive, all right. So he must be dreaming, then. That was what last night had been. A dream. Reluctantly he opened his eyes, knowing the dream would be over the second he did.

The bed was empty, and a disappointment so intense pulsed through his body he slammed his eyes shut again. But the scent was there. Her scent. Feminine and seductive. It *was* Annie. And she had been here.

He opened his eyes again and sat up, running a hand through his hair as he glanced around the room. There was no sign of her, but still he felt her, felt her vibrant energy shimmering as clearly as if she was lying beside him.

He wanted her here, right here. With him. Now.

He smelled the coffee then and knew she was in the kitchen.

Panic gripped him. What would he say? What *could* he say? *Gee, thanks, Annie. It was swell.*

He tugged on a pair of jeans, cursing himself the entire time. He'd cut off his right arm before he'd hurt Annie, and now look what he'd done. The sound of eggs frying and the smell of bacon assaulted him, and as he made his way to the kitchen, he also realized he was starving.

She was bent over, peering into the refrigerator. His heart slammed in his chest at the sight of her. She was wearing one of his shirts, and it skimmed the top of her thighs; her long legs were bare. She couldn't have been sexier if she'd had on a skimpy negligee.

His body responded instantly, and he groaned inwardly. How the hell was he going to get through this if he couldn't even look at her without getting hard?

She turned then and saw him. He saw the flicker of fear in her eyes, but then she smiled and looked quickly away.

"Good morning." She pulled an orange-juice container out of the refrigerator and then shut the door.

"Mornin'."

"I thought you might be hungry." She set the juice down and turned her attention to the eggs. "I hope fried eggs are all right."

"Fine."

This was crazy, Jared thought. They'd just spent the night together, and they were talking like strangers. He watched as she removed the eggs from the pan, put them on a plate with some bacon and set it in front of him.

That was when he noticed her hand was shaking.

"Annie..." He sighed heavily and reached for her hand, but she yanked it away as if he'd burned her.

"Don't you say it, Jared Stone." Her voice was low and hard. "Don't you dare say 'I'm sorry,' or, 'This should have never happened.' If you do, so help me, you're going to be wearing these eggs, instead of eating them."

Stunned, he simply stared at her.

"Last night was the most incredible night of my life," she said quietly, her voice wavering. "Don't take that away from me."

Her words made his heart jump. Desperately he wanted to believe her, to pull her into his arms and drag her back in the bedroom, so he could unbutton that shirt slowly and see every inch of her in the daylight. Hold her close, laugh with her, love her... His hands clenched into fists.

He couldn't.

"Annie, my God..." He hadn't a clue what to say. But what was the difference? She'd hate him no matter what he said. "Look, emotions were running pretty high last night. I took advantage of that."

She shook her head. "You took advantage of nothing, Jared. We're both adults. I knew exactly what I was doing."

"I scared you half to death at the rig," he argued. "You thought I was..."

The sentence died on his tongue. He shut his eyes and shook his head.

"Say it, Jared." She placed her hands on the counter separating them. Her eyes flashed with anger. "Say it."

A fist tightened around his chest as he lifted his gaze to hers. "You thought I was Jonathan."

Her eyes narrowed. "That's what this is about, isn't it? Not just that I thought you were Jonathan at the rig, but that I thought you were Jonathan in bed last night."

He wanted to slam his fist into the wall or kick down the door. Anything to release the horrendous pressure building inside him.

"I want you to look at me, Jared." When he stared at the wall behind her, she curled her fingers into fists and banged them on the counter. "Look at me, dammit!"

Jaw tight, he did as she asked. If she'd been angry before, she was furious now. And so was he. He just didn't understand why.

She leaned closer and he heard the struggle in her voice to stay calm. "Last night there was no one on that couch or in that bed or in my mind except you. You, and only you. Do you understand that? Not physically, emotionally or mentally."

She turned away from the counter, jammed her hands on her hips, then spun back around. Her eyes glistened. "I loved Jonathan. You loved Jonathan. But we can't bring him back. We can only be thankful we had the time with him that we did."

Jared swallowed down the tightness in his throat. Still he said nothing.

"I didn't come here looking for this." Her shoulders sagged. "It just happened. And I'm glad it happened. I'm only sorry that you aren't."

She didn't understand, he thought, his chest aching. How could he ever make her understand?

"Annie," he said hoarsely, "he . . . he was my brother. He loved you. He should be with you. I have no right."

She sighed wearily, and the pain in her eyes was like a knife in his gut.

"So what shall we do, Jared? Shall we be friends?"

Friends? He frowned.

"Or maybe I should just think of you as a brother?" The sarcasm dripped from her words. "Is that how we should see each other, Jared? Brother and sister?"

She was being ridiculous, but her point was made. After last night, he'd never think of her as a friend, and he sure as hell would never think of her as a sister.

Dammit, he didn't know what to think anymore.

"Annie," he said quietly, "there's something else. We...I..." He raked his hands through his hair. "Dammit, I didn't use any protection last night."

Her cheeks flushed. She turned to the sink and stared out the window.

"It was careless of me," he said awkwardly. "But you don't have to worry, I mean, about me. I've been no saint, but I've always used something with every woman I've ever been with."

She drew in a slow breath and turned back to face him. "You don't have to worry about me, either," she said, but there was no expression on her face. "Jonathan is the only other man I've ever made love to."

He stared at her. She'd never been with anyone but Jonathan? A rush of elation poured through him, followed closely by a rush of pain. Had she loved Jonathan so much no one else had ever compared?

Until she'd met up with Jonathan's twin brother?

He stared at the food in front of him and wanted to smash the plate into a thousand pieces. "And if you're pregnant?"

She was quiet for what seemed like an eternity. "It's highly unlikely, but why don't we worry about that if it happens?"

He hated himself, because the idea of her having his baby brought a spark of joy to the emptiness inside him.

And at the same time, he had to pray it wouldn't happen. "When will you know?"

Her face tightened. "Don't worry about it, Jared. No one's going to get the shotgun."

"That's not what I mean, dammit," he said tightly, then added more gently, "I care, Annie."

She sighed, then tossed her head in frustration. "About three weeks. Just about the time we finish drilling, and before I have to leave."

Leave. No matter what the outcome with the well, she did have to leave. She'd get on with her life, and he with his.

They were both quiet as they ate breakfast. He was no longer hungry, but he forced himself. She picked at a piece of toast and sipped at her coffee. When they finished, they both dressed and drove into town silently together to give Slater and the crew the good news.

They had an oil well waiting to be drilled.

Eight

"I swear, he was the most gorgeous man I'd ever seen. Right off the cover of Handsome Hunks Illustrated. Wavy sun-streaked hair, big brown eyes and quarterback shoulders. I fell in love instantly."

Annie looked up from the menu she'd been studying and smiled as she listened to Jessica describe the shoe salesman she'd met in San Antonio.

Between school and work the past three years, Annie had spent little time with friends. It felt good to be out with another woman, exchanging girl-talk. Especially after the past three days of drilling. Everything had gone smoothly since they'd started work again, but Jared had been irritable, and the tension between them had been almost palpable. Annie had welcomed Jessica's invitation to lunch.

"And then he turned around—" Jessica leaned forward, her blue eyes wide as she whispered "—and I was a goner. He had the most perfect butt I've ever seen."

Annie laughed at Jessica's outrageous comment. "You mean to tell me you really looked at his, uh, posterior?"

The waitress, a pretty brunette, appeared then and set two iced teas on the table. "First thing I always look at," the brunette said as casually as if they'd been discussing an item on the menu.

Annie shook her head and reached for her tea, resisting the urge to ask what the second thing she looked at might be.

"Don't tell me you haven't noticed Jared's," Jessica said to Annie with a mischievous grin. "He's adorable."

Annie nearly choked on her tea. Adorable? Somehow, she couldn't quite put that word to Jared. Nor could she imagine having this conversation with Jessica and a strange woman. She felt her cheeks heat.

"Jared," the waitress nodded with approval. "Now there's a *fine* specimen of—"

"I'll have a chicken salad," Annie said quickly, cutting the woman off.

"Me, too." Jessica handed the menu back to the waitress and wiggled her eyebrows. "Hold the dressing."

Laughing, the brunette walked away. Jessica looked at Annie and grinned. "I mention Jared, and you turn red as a beet. So what's the skinny with you two?"

Annie doubted she'd ever met anyone more forthright than Jessica. She had a simple enthusiastic outlook on life that could charm the most hardened of individuals. And while it was a pleasure on one hand, the unexpected turn this conversation had taken was anything but.

"There is no skinny." Annie busied herself squeezing a lemon into her tea. She hated lemon, but anything to keep busy so she didn't have to look at Jessica. "I'm here to work, that's it."

Jessica's laugh was so enchanting that Annie noticed several men sitting at the counter turn and stare with interest.

"And I'm Bugs Bunny." She wrinkled her nose. "I've seen the way you two look at each other. If you could bottle that heat, there'd be a new source for world energy."

If Annie's cheeks had been warm before, they were on fire now. What was the point in denial? Jessica would see right through it, anyway. And besides, it felt good to talk to another woman, even if that woman was Jared's sister.

She sighed and stirred the ice in her tea. "Is it really that obvious?"

"Like sequins on a saddle," Jessica drawled.

Without warning, Annie's eyes began to burn. She blinked and looked away.

"Annie, hey." Jessica's voice softened as she reached across the table and laid her hand over Annie's. "What's the matter?"

Annie shook her head. She was making a fool of herself in front of Jessica. "Nothing. I'm fine, really."

"No, you're not." Jessica frowned. "It's Jared, isn't it? He's not making this easy. I swear, that man is too damn stubborn for his own good, or anyone's else's, for that matter."

Annie's laugh was dry. "It didn't take long to figure that one out."

"That was always one of the differences between Jonathan and Jared, you know," Jessica said. "You could talk to Jonathan, reason with him. With Jared, you always needed a sledgehammer."

At the mention of Jonathan, Annie felt a knot tighten in her stomach. How could she, after being engaged to Jonathan, be casually sitting here discussing Jared with Jessica?

Annie stared down at her hands in her lap. "Jessica, this is so awkward. You must think I'm ... well, that I ..."

"I don't think anything of you, Annie," Jessica said softly, "except that you're a terrific person and you have great taste in men. There was never any question that you loved Jonathan. Everyone knows you did."

Jessica's eyes were bright now as she tightened her fingers around Annie's. "But no matter how much we miss him, no matter how much we want him back, it's not possible. More than anyone, Jonathan would want you and Jared to be happy. Shoot—" she wiped at the corner of her eye "—knowing Jonathan, I'll bet he arranged this whole thing."

The two women looked at each other and smiled, then laughed. A weight that Annie hadn't even realized she'd been carrying around suddenly lifted. It didn't ease the pain, but she felt considerably lighter.

"So what do I do now?" she asked Jessica. "He blames himself for Jonathan's death. Every time he looks at me, that's all he sees."

"Like I said, he's a stubborn man. Give him some time, and if that doesn't work, get yourself a sledgehammer. He'll come around."

Annie wasn't so sure. But the idea of a sledgehammer appealed greatly to her. "I think you're going to need one for yourself when you move out to that ghost town of yours. Jared and Jake have both threatened to drop you down a well and leave you there until you come to your senses."

Jessica grinned. "Oh, they'll try, all right, but stubborn doesn't stop with those two. I'm afraid I inherited that character flaw myself. They've been hovering over me since our mother died, questioning every date I've ever been on, watching every step I take."

"How old were you when your mother died?" Annie asked.

"Fourteen," she answered, then stared down at her iced tea. "I ran a little wild after that, especially after my father married Myrna." Her grin was wicked. "I admit, I delighted in tormenting the woman. She hadn't a clue how to deal with a rebellious teenager. She was easy to get around, but three big brothers, on the other hand, were a little more difficult. They were breathing down my neck constantly. Despite all their efforts, I came close to getting into some serious trouble."

"What kind of trouble?"

"Even in a town this small, there were drugs and liquor. I was so lonely and I missed my mother so much I could have gone that way, but fate intervened and I turned everything around."

Annie leaned forward intently. "Fate?"

The waitress brought their salads then. Jessica just smiled. "It's another story for another time. But let's just say that Makeshift—that's my ghost town—saved my life. No matter what Jared or Jake think, nothing would ever hurt me there. It's the safest place in the world. Whether they like it or not, I'm moving out there and building my youth center."

Annie recognized the rigid tilt of Jessica's chin and lift of her shoulders. It was the Stone trademark of tenacity. She'd be moving out there, all right. No doubt about it.

Jessica grinned. "Wait till you see the fuss Jake and Jared are going to make. It's going to be great."

An ache spread through Annie's chest. "I wish I could, Jessica. But I'm afraid I won't be here. Once we finish drilling, I'll be going back home."

Jessica looked at her and smiled reassuringly. "Don't be too sure about that, Annie. Jared might be stubborn, but he's not stupid. He won't let you go."

He'd not only let her go, Annie thought bleakly, he'd hold the door for her. But for this moment, as Annie looked into Jessica's confident eyes, she felt a tiny ray of hope. It wasn't much, but when it came to Jared Stone, she'd take whatever she could get.

"Of course I'm sure."

Annie switched the phone from one ear to the other as she dug under the mountain of paperwork for her pencil. She'd had it in her hand just before her supervisor from Arloco, Ken Fisher, had called, but now it had mysteriously disappeared.

"Like I told you yesterday, Ken," she said, flipping through a stack of logs, "and the day before that, everything is fine. An overzealous civil servant is not a problem, and we've made up the time, anyway. We've been drilling seven days and we're not even off the projected depth by five feet."

Of course, she didn't mention that the pipes had twisted off once in the past four days and the lights had blown twice. Ken really didn't need that pressure. He'd have enough when he got the bill for the overtime they'd had to pay when three of the men had come down with flu.

Only half listening as her supervisor continued to grill her on the well's progress, Annie lifted the corner of the map she'd been working on. The pencil rolled out, then over the side and under the desk. Exasperated, she juggled the phone between her shoulder and chin while she knelt down to retrieve it, but only succeeded in dragging the entire phone off the desk. It crashed to the floor.

She bit back the swear word on her tongue and got on her hands and knees.

"What's the big deal?" She scooted under the big metal desk and searched the floor. "We've worked on dozens of projects like this and you're never this concerned, especially so early in a project. Is there something you aren't telling me?"

Where had that pencil gone now? she thought irritably. Wasn't there even one thing in her life she had some control over? Was a pencil going to get the best of her, too?

Teeth set, she squinted and scanned the dark cubicle under the desk.

"A baby!" She jerked upward at the news and hit her head on the underside of the desk.

"Oh, Ken, that's wonderful," she said softly, rubbing her head. "When?"

Still under the desk, she leaned forward and sat cross-legged, listening intently while he gave her the details. Annie knew Ken's wife, Debbie, and she knew how long they'd been trying to conceive. That certainly explained why the man was on edge.

"Look, don't worry about me," she told him when he'd finished. "I'm a big girl, remember? I can take care of everything here, okay? Okay. And don't call me, I'll call you."

Smiling, she hung up the phone. Ken Fisher was going to be a daddy. He'd sounded excited, but scared to death. She sighed softly and pulled her knees up, resting her cheek on them, closing her eyes as she gently touched her own stomach, wondering...

"You want to tell me what the hell that was all about?"

Startled, her eyes flew open, but all she saw were a pair of boots plastered with mud and two denim-covered legs.

She craned her head and met Jared's dark gaze as he stared down at her.

"What was what all about?" She started to move out from under the desk, but he sat in the desk chair and moved closer, trapping her.

"That phone call. I heard you."

She frowned up at him. He'd been ornery as a grizzly bear all week. He'd also been working extra shifts and obviously getting little sleep. His eyes looked like American flags and fatigue lined his brow. If she hadn't been so worried about him, she'd be furious. A mixture of frustration and exhaustion coursed through her.

"Jared," she said with a sigh, "just say whatever it is that's on your mind. I have work to do."

His lips thinned. "Are you pregnant?"

"What!"

"I heard you talking just now. I want to know if you're pregnant."

So that was what it was. He'd been watching her closely all week, and she'd had a feeling this was the reason. As if by just looking at her he could tell if she was going to have a baby.

"Eavesdropping, Jared?" She clucked her tongue. "Shame on you."

He scowled at her. "Annie, I have a right to know."

"Yes, Jared, you do."

"Well?"

"Well, what?" She folded her arms.

"Are you pregnant?"

Jared knew he was shouting but was too angry to care. When he'd walked in and heard bits and pieces of Annie's conversation—under the desk, no less—he'd felt a jolt of excitement when he'd heard the word "baby," then a rage when she'd said she'd "take care of it."

"It's been exactly one week." Her lips thinned in annoyance. "How could I possibly know if I was pregnant or not?"

He thought about that. "I thought women knew stuff like that."

She twisted under the desk and faced him. "That only proves how little you know about women, Jared Stone. Now let me out of here."

He didn't. "Well, what am I supposed to think? I find you hiding under the desk, you said 'baby,' then you said you'd 'take care of it.'"

She looked up at him, and the pain and hurt he saw there made him instantly regret his words.

"Is that what you think, Jared?" she said quietly. "That I might do that if I were pregnant?"

He felt like a jerk. Hell, he *was* a jerk. He knew she would never do that. Not Annie.

He let out a long breath and shook his head. "I'm sorry. I'm just a little testy right now."

"A *little* testy?" Her laugh was sarcastic. "Buddy, of all the men I've ever worked with, you get the trophy for testy."

She was right. He had been difficult. But this past week had been hell. Since the permit fiasco, they'd already had more than their share of problems, with the crew getting sick and equipment breaking down. He'd worked long hours, not only to make up the slack with the crew, but to keep himself occupied every minute he could. It was either that or think about Annie, and that was one luxury he couldn't allow himself. He'd kept a close eye on her all week, but unless they needed to discuss the operation of the rig, he'd managed to stay away from her.

But the nights. Damn, it was the nights that nearly did him in. He'd dream of those legs wrapped around him, her fingers splayed over his body, and he'd wake up in a sweat, his body tight with desire. It was all he could do not to drive into town and drag her back out here with him.

He looked down at her now, at her long lithe body folded neatly under the desk, and felt a strong urge to pull her onto his lap and kiss that soft honey-sweet mouth.

That was when he happened to look up and see Slater standing in the doorway, leaning casually against the doorjamb. The big man had a grin on his face that set Jared's teeth on edge.

"Hi, Jared. Who you talkin' to?"

Jared groaned silently, wondering not only how much Slater had heard, but realizing how *strange* the situation looked at the moment.

"Oh, my God!" Annie squeaked. "Please tell me that wasn't Slater I just heard."

"Oh, hi, Bailey," Slater piped up. "I didn't see you down there."

Exasperated, Annie shoved Jared, sending the desk chair careering backward. She unfolded herself from beneath the desk and stood, her hands on her hips, as she glared first at Jared, then at Slater.

"I lost my pencil," she said to Slater, daring him to dispute it.

He gestured innocently, but said nothing. *For once, a wise man,* Annie thought irritably. *Unlike some men.*

"And you, Jared Stone—" her voice lowered fiercely "—*if* I have something to tell you, I'll tell you *when* I'm ready. In the meantime, stop watching me like I'm some kind of a goldfish in a bowl."

Jared started to say something, then slammed his mouth shut and looked at Slater, who was grinning at Annie.

"Was there something you wanted?" Jared growled at his foreman.

"Oh, yeah." Slater turned his attention to Jared. "Pipes twisted off again. Glenn's going to refit, but we'll have to shut down while we do."

"That's the second time this week!" Jared jumped out of the chair and sent it toppling over. He stormed out of the office, spewing expletives.

Annie shook her head and frowned. "Charming."

Slater laughed and moved into the office. He picked up the chair and gestured for Annie to sit.

"There've been a lot of problems," she said as she lowered herself into the chair.

With a shrug, Slater sat on the edge of the desk. "Nothing we can't handle."

"I sure hope you're right." She twisted her neck to loosen the knot forming between her shoulders.

"They giving you a lot of heat from the top?"

"No."

He narrowed his eyes as he leaned back and studied her. "Have you told them?"

How could one man be so intuitive and another—she stared out the office window—so dense? "I will."

"I see." He glanced down at the maps and logs on her desk. "How you coming with that?"

She stared at the paperwork and slowly shook her head. "I've remapped everything Jonathan worked up. He's right on, yet still, I have the feeling that something is missing."

"You have all the seismics and logs?"

"Everything that Jonathan had. It's almost as if . . ."

She hesitated, unsure of what she wanted to say. She lifted her gaze to Slater's.

"As if he wasn't done?" Slater said.

"Yes." She nodded thoughtfully. "As if he wasn't done."

Slater reached over and took Annie's hand in his. His palms were rough and callused, but she was surprised how gentle the big man's touch was.

"He left a lot of things unfinished," Slater said. "You were one of them."

A familiar ache tightened her stomach. "We aren't talking about me."

He shrugged. "You're just part of it, Bailey. A lot of things were left unsettled when Jonathan died."

That was what Jared was, she realized. Unsettled. He'd lost a brother and his dream at the same time, then separated himself from his family when he'd gone to South America.

"What about you, Slater? You were Jonathan's friend. You didn't come to the funeral."

His fingers tightened on her hand, then he let go and sat back with a sigh. "We said our goodbyes."

She stared at him curiously, wondering what he meant by that. The sound of Jared yelling at one of the crew distracted her. Jared hadn't said goodbye, she realized. Not to Jonathan, or his father. No matter how angry he'd been with J.T., Annie knew that Jared had loved him.

"Slater," she said, "do you think Jared's father was wrong to shut the rig down after Jonathan died?"

"I've never been one to judge another man's actions, Bailey. J.T. took Jonathan's death hard, and he decided he'd rather have an angry son, than another dead one. Jared wasn't thinking too clearly himself. He said some things that were better left unsaid."

"And then he went to Venezuela."

"He joined a company that had a reputation for taking on the jobs that no one else would. Dangerous jobs. It was more like he'd joined a war. I went down there for a while just to keep an eye on him. He came back to the States a few months after I did."

"When J.T. died," she said quietly.

Slater nodded. "Everyone thought J.T. would outlive us all. It was one more crate added to that load Jared's carrying on those shoulders of his."

"His father loved him," Annie said. "I only met the man once, but it was obvious how proud J.T. was of all his children."

"That he was," Slater agreed.

And he had good reason to be, Annie thought. The Stone siblings were strong, independent, hardworking people who loved deeply. She was going to miss them.

One of them in particular.

"Excuse me."

Both Slater and Annie turned. Glenn Woods stood in the doorway.

"Do you have any aspirin?" he asked.

"Is that flu still bothering you?" Annie asked, reaching into the top desk drawer.

He shook his head. "No, I'm fine. Just a headache."

Slater frowned at the young man. "My head would hurt, too, if I'd lost my paycheck in a card game last night."

Glenn shrugged sheepishly and moved into the office. "Just a friendly game with some boys in town. I'll win it back."

"You'd be way ahead if you didn't try," Slater warned, but Annie sensed that the advice was falling on deaf ears.

She pulled the cap off the small plastic bottle in her hand and tipped it sideways, preparing to count out two tablets.

What she wasn't prepared for was the sudden explosion that threw her to the floor.

Nine

——

The trailer shook from the force of the blast. A framed map flew off the wall, shattering on the floor. Annie felt two strong arms reach under her and lift her as if she were no more than a feather.

"You okay?" Slater asked.

When she nodded yes, he deposited her in the desk chair, then turned and ran out of the trailer, yelling before his boots even hit the dirt. Glenn shot a worried look at her, then followed Slater. She rose on shaking knees to follow them, but fell back when the room began to spin. She touched her fingers to her temple and felt the wetness there. Stunned, she pulled her hand away and stared at the blood on her fingers.

What the hell had happened?

The shouts of the men outside drew her out of her daze.

Jared.

Adrenaline shot through her. Her heart hammered in her chest as she flew from her chair and tore out of the office. The smell of burned oil hung in the air, and the crew scrambled around, two of them working the fire hose while two others struggled with a wrench to shut off the pipe leading from the compressor—or at least what *had* been the compressor. The tank had ruptured, and there was a gaping hole in its side. Pieces of metal and air hose littered the ground.

Jared. Where's Jared?

Frantically she searched for him, but all she saw was Slater, who was kneeling on the ground behind the compressor. Two other men were beside him, bent over and staring down.

Jared.

"Oh, God, no. *No!*"

It was a dream, a horrible nightmare. She ran toward him, and it seemed as if she moved in slow motion. Slater was directing a man to get some cold water and a towel as she dropped down beside Jared. He was lying on the ground. Blood and dirt streaked his face and neck, and on his forehead was an angry gash.

"Jared," she called to him, leaning close. Her hand shook as she touched his arm.

He was so still. She swallowed the sob in her throat and ran her hand over his chest. "Jared!"

He stirred then, and his eyes slowly opened. Relief washed through her and she touched his cheek, calling his name again. He blinked several times, then tried to raise himself.

Slater eased him back down. "Whoa, there, buddy. You just lie still."

Annie took the water and towel handed her, then gently washed Jared's face.

He winced when he lifted his arm and touched his fore-head. "What the...?"

"The compressor decided to play slam ball with your head," Slater said. "Fortunately for you, you've got a hard one."

Slater was smiling, but Annie saw the fear in the big man's eyes. This had been close. Way too close. She looked up at Glenn, who was standing next to her, his face white. "Glenn, bring my car. We've got to get him to the doctor in town."

"I'm fine." Jared tried to raise himself up on one elbow again, but fell back. "I don't need—"

"Not one word, Jared Stone," Annie threatened. "You're going if I have to hog-tie you. And in your condition, I'd like to see you stop me."

"And me," Slater added.

Jared frowned at the pair of them, then sucked in a sharp breath as he struggled to sit. "I go on one condition," he said haltingly. "Slater stays here...gets the backup compressor hooked up while the crew finishes repairing the twisted pipe."

"Jared, for God's sake..." Annie started to argue.

He reached out and took hold of her arm. Even in his weakened condition the fingers that curled around her arm were strong.

"I mean it, Annie," he said hoarsely. "You can take me, but everyone else keeps working."

Determination glinted through the pain in his eyes. Frustrated, Annie looked at Slater. He nodded reluctantly.

"I'll go get a blanket," the foreman said grimly. "We can lower the back seat of your Cherokee and lay him out."

When Slater left, Jared drew Annie close to him. "You're bleeding." He reached up to touch her forehead.

"It's nothing." She brushed his hand away and touched the damp cloth to his neck. "I just bumped my head. I don't want you to think about me."

He stared at her for a long moment, then his eyelids grew heavy and he leaned against her. "I always think about you, Annie," he said weakly. "Always."

He slumped against her then and his eyes drifted closed while he was still murmuring her name.

It was dark when he opened his eyes. His head hurt like hell, and his shoulder felt as if he'd been kicked by a mule. He thought for a moment he must have really tied one on, but then the events of the previous afternoon—the explosion followed by the trip to the doctor—came crashing back, and all he could do was groan.

He was in his bed, dressed in a pair of sweatpants. He sat up slowly, then waited until the throbbing in his head eased. The ticking of the clock on the bedside table was like the drumming of a rock band. He squinted, trying to focus on the lighted dial, but the numbers blurred together.

Damn. He knew he'd gotten off easy, especially considering how close he'd been standing to the compressor when it had let loose. If the piece of metal that had sliced into his back had been ten inches higher, he probably wouldn't be sitting here at all. The doctor had told him that he should consider himself lucky that all he had was a few stitches in his shoulder and a mild concussion.

Lucky. Yeah. Right.

Dragging a hand through his hair, he blinked several times and stared at the clock again. It was two-thirty in the morning and he was wide awake. He thought seriously about going to the rig, but Annie, he knew, was asleep on the couch, and she'd already threatened to shut the rig down if he stepped one foot out of bed. She not only *could* do it, he knew she *would*. He recognized that determined set to her shoulders and chin only too well.

He was stuck here for the next two days, as per doctor's orders. Like a prisoner. And between Annie and Slater, there was no hope for a reprieve. All he could do was wait.

The damn ticking of the clock pounded away at his patience like a hammer. He felt like murdering something, so it might as well be a clock, he decided irritably. He reached for the offending timepiece, then hurled it across the room.

The reward for his foolishness was a sharp stab of pain in his shoulder. He held his breath, then slowly let it out.

The clock kept ticking.

What the hell was he supposed to do at this hour of the night? He was going to go crazy if he had to just sit here.

He thought of Annie, asleep in the other room, and he couldn't help but smile. She'd driven like a bat out of hell to get him to the doctor's office yesterday afternoon, then acted like a mother tiger with a wounded cub when she checked him in, harassing the nurse when she didn't move fast enough and pestering the doctor with a hundred questions. If Jared hadn't been in so much pain at the time, he might have been amused.

Annie Bailey was a determined woman, he thought now with a sigh. A determined beautiful sexy woman. Not a minute had gone by since they'd made love that he hadn't wanted her again, in his arms, in his bed. The only thing that had eased the tension was work.

And now he didn't even have that.

He gripped the sheet in his fist, and despite the feeling that a truck had run over him, he felt desire rise in him. He needed to touch her, have her body against his, her—

"Jared?"

Her whisper startled him. He hadn't heard her come into the room. It was nearly pitch-black, so he couldn't even see her.

He didn't answer her, just twisted the sheet in his hand and ground his teeth, hoping she wouldn't see he was awake.

She moved into the room. "Jared, are you all right?"

He still didn't answer her. When the mattress dipped beside him, he stifled a groan. He felt as if the door on his cell had just closed. There was nowhere to go, nowhere to run. She was too close. Too damn close.

"I just knocked the clock over. Go back to bed."

"Are you in pain?"

Pain? He almost laughed at the thought. If he was in ten times the physical pain, it would be nothing compared to the pain of wanting this woman and knowing he could never have her.

She reached across him to turn on the light, but he stopped her. If she saw him, she'd know how much he wanted her. He couldn't bear that. "I'm fine, Annie."

"I'm supposed to check on you," she said softly. "Because of the concussion."

"I'm still breathing."

"Do you want a pain pill? It's been a few hours and—"

"*No*. I don't want anything. *Just go.*"

She was quiet for a moment; the only sound was that damn clock. He hadn't wanted to be so terse, but he was in a corner. *Annie, go... please... just go...*

He felt the mattress shift and thought she was leaving. He groaned when she moved closer to him.

"I can't," she said, and he heard the misery in her voice.

"Oh, God, Annie..."

He closed his eyes and turned away from her, but he could still smell the scent of his soap drifting from her skin. She'd showered earlier and he'd never wanted to be a bar of soap so badly in his life. But it was *her* scent that closed around him and drew him back like silken fingers. Her own soft feminine scent that made him want to wrap his body around hers and never let go.

"When I saw you earlier lying on the ground, I thought that you were... that you..."

Her voice broke. With a murmured curse, he turned back around and gathered her close. "Annie, I'm fine," he said gently. "I really am. It would take a hell of a lot more than a little flying metal to do me in."

She'd been an idiot to come in here like this, Annie told herself. He was going to be all right, the doctor had assured her repeatedly. But she couldn't erase from her mind that horrible image of him lying on the ground, and the terror she'd felt when she thought he might have been dead. She turned her cheek to his chest, wanting to hear the beating of his heart.

"How's your head?" he asked, combing the hair away from her face.

The tender stroking of his fingers on her face relaxed her, and the heat of his bare chest warmed her through her thin cotton robe. "I told you, it's just a scratch."

"So you did."

Her heart skipped when his lips brushed the top of her head. His hand slid caressingly over her arm, and the sensation sent ripples of liquid heat coursing through her. "Jared, I didn't come in here to... I mean, I didn't expect or want you to..."

"To what?" He touched his lips to her temple.

She lifted her head. It was too dark to see his face, but she smelled the musky scent of his skin and the faint aroma of antiseptic.

"I wanted to be next to you, to know that you're all right." Her fingers tightened on his arm. "Jared," she said raggedly, "you...you could have died."

Jared felt Annie tremble in his arms, and he cursed himself for wanting her as he did right now. He'd been so wrapped up in feeling sorry for himself that he couldn't be at the rig he'd nearly forgotten what *she* must have gone through. All the old feelings for Jonathan that must have resurfaced.

An ache spread through him that had nothing to do with his injuries. It might be the hardest thing he'd ever done in his life, but he could do this for her. For Jonathan.

He laid back on the bed and pulled her with him. "I didn't die, Annie. I'm here and I'm fine. Just lie here with me."

"No." She started to pull away. "You're hurt, and I can't—"

"No, I don't mean that." He tugged her gently back. "We both need to sleep, and I don't feel right knowing you're on the couch."

"I don't mind," she protested, and tried to rise again.

"I mind." He wrapped an arm around her and brought her flush against him, her back to his chest. She drew in a sharp breath at the feel of his arousal against her buttocks.

He sighed heavily. "Look, Annie, I'm not going to lie and tell you I don't want to make love to you. It's pretty damn obvious I do. But I'm not going to do anything about it. I want you here. With me. Just for tonight."

Annie desperately wanted to turn in Jared's arms and touch him, reassure herself that he was fine, that he was alive. But if she did, it would be like lighting a match to dry kindling. They were both aroused, not only from the closeness, but from the tension they'd been holding in. Her body screamed for release.

But she couldn't. She couldn't make love with Jared knowing that he thought of it as "just for tonight." She'd been through that once already.

She let herself relax against him, almost smiling at the thought that they were actually going to *sleep* together. He seemed to relax, too, and lightly pressed his lips to the back of her head.

"Get some sleep, Annie."

His arm tightened around her, pulling her closer still, fitting their bodies like two pieces of a puzzle. She let her eyes drift closed, refusing to think about how close she'd come to losing him. He *was* still here, she thought. His strong muscular body pressed against hers was proof of that.

And her last thought, before exhaustion finally won over, was how much she loved the man who was holding her.

"Dammit, Jared, why the hell didn't you call me yesterday when this happened?"

Annie watched as Jake, his hands on his hips, stood glaring down at his brother stretched out on the couch.

"It wasn't—"

"I told him to." Annie interjected. She was standing beside Jake, her arms crossed. "He said there was no reason to bother you."

"Bother me! Bother your own brother? I have to hear this from Tom at the feed store while I'm picking up a load of grain this morning?" Jake threw his arms out in disgust. "And just wait until Jessica gets the message I left on her machine. She'll give you a shiner to match the one you've already got."

Jared frowned. "Look, it's no big—"

"And why are you dressed in work boots and jeans?" Jake asked, narrowing his eyes. He looked at Annie. "He didn't try to go to the rig, did he?"

She nodded. "Tried to sneak out while I was in the bathroom. Couldn't get far without these, though." She pulled Jared's truck keys out of her pocket.

Jared's lips thinned. "I was only going outside for some fresh air."

"Yeah. That's why I found you in the truck, swearing loud enough to rattle the windows."

Annie moved into the kitchen to pour Jake a cup of coffee. She was glad he'd shown up when he had. Jared was a terrible patient; she was weary of arguing with the stubborn fool and was glad to let someone else take over.

He'd pretended to be asleep when she'd woken up that morning. She'd slipped quietly out of bed, not wanting to disturb him, and gone into the bathroom. That was when he'd dressed and tried to make his escape.

He was furious that she'd second-guessed him.

She was furious that he'd tried something so stupid.

They'd been arguing ever since.

With a sigh, she moved back into the living room and handed Jake his coffee. He thanked her, then turned back to Jared. "So, you want to tell me what happened?"

"I was standing a little too close to the compressor when it decided to attempt a moon launch."

"The compressor blew?" Jake frowned. "Compressors don't blow."

"Not usually."

There was a tense silence as the two brothers stared at each other. Annie glanced from Jared to Jake. "What are you saying? That someone tampered with the compressor?"

Jared winced as he sat up. "We aren't saying anything just yet."

"You're implying something," she said.

"It's probably nothing." Jake gazed thoughtfully at his coffee, then looked at Jared. "Have you had any other problems?"

"Permits lost, pipe twisting off, lights blowing. Nothing completely out of line, just more than normal."

"Enough to throw you off schedule and out of budget, though, right?"

Jared nodded grimly.

Jake began to prowl the room. "It's sounding a little too familiar to me."

"What sounds familiar?" Annie asked, frustrated at the sudden quiet in the room. At least when they were arguing, she knew what was going on.

Jared reached for his own cup of coffee on the end table. "Jake had some problems a few months ago with an ex-employee cutting fence and messing with the watering pumps. It was subtle, but effective. He nearly lost the ranch."

"I nearly lost Emma and Savannah." Jake's face went rigid. "They were in the barn when the bastard set it on fire."

"Oh, my God," Annie whispered. "What happened?"

"I got them out in time." Jake stared hard at his coffee cup. A muscle jumped in his jaw. "Just barely."

Her knees felt weak and she sank down on the couch beside Jared. "Why would anyone do such a thing?"

"He was angry because I'd fired him, and the only job he could find was driving for Myrna."

"You mean, like a chauffeur?"

"Yeah." Jake took a sip of his coffee. "I suppose that's enough to make anyone crazy."

Annie certainly couldn't argue with him there. "Jared, isn't it suspicious that Jake had problems when Myrna wanted his land, and now you're having problems when she wants yours?"

Jared shot Jake a look, and it was apparent that the thought had occurred to both of them.

"No." Jared shook his head. "I didn't believe it then, and I can't believe it now. Myrna's capable of a lot of things, but not this."

"No one has better reason than me to dislike the woman," Jake said. "She's selfish, obnoxious and condescending. But I still can't imagine her going this far."

"What about that man, the ex-employee?" she asked.

"He's in Midland Correctional for a long time," Jake said coldly. "He knows better than to ever show his face around here again."

Based on Jake's murderous expression, Annie thought, the man was lucky to even be alive.

"So we're at a dead end," she said with a sigh and leaned back on the couch. It was still warm from Jared's body.

"Look," Jared said, "there's really no reason for us to believe that these mishaps were anything other than just that. Let's forget about it and—"

The door burst open and Jessica walked in, both arms full of overflowing grocery bags. Jake hurried over and relieved her of the bags, then set them in the kitchen. Her eyes were flashing as she stalked across the room to Jared.

"Jared Alexander Stone, how dare you not call me and tell me you were hurt." She stood in front of him, her arms folded as she glared at him.

Jared rolled his head back and groaned. "I'm fine."

"Oh, sure. You look fine. Black and blue are definitely your colors. Don't you think so, Annie?"

Annie studied his face thoughtfully. "The purple is nice, too."

And then Jessica was in Jared's arms, hugging him even as she continued to scold him. "You scared the hell out of me, Jared," she said more softly, pulling back so she could look at him. "Are you sure you're all right? No broken bones? No internal bleeding?"

"I'm fine. Really," he reassured her. "Just a couple of stitches in my shoulder."

Jessica let out a breath and looked at Annie. "You okay?"

Annie nodded. "Except for the ten years' life I lost and a small scratch."

"Hey, Jessie," Jake called from the kitchen, "what do you want me to do with this stuff?" He held up a small plastic bag labeled Cactus Flat Pharmacy.

Jessica gave Jared a kiss on his cheek, then stood. She glanced at Annie and rolled her eyes. "Men are so helpless."

"Don't forget stubborn and obstinate," Annie added, which only earned her a frown from Jared.

"Goes without saying." Jessica turned to Jake. "Throw it over here."

The bag sailed across the room. Jessica caught it easily and tossed it to Jared.

He caught the bag. "What *is* all this stuff?"

She pushed up the sleeves of her white cotton shirt and headed for the kitchen. "I thought you might need a few things. You being incapacitated and all. Food, aspirin, bandages. A few other essentials."

"I am *not* incapacitated," he called after her, and peered into the bag. "*Jessie…*"

"What?" She smiled innocently.

Jared scowled darkly.

"I'm starving." Jessica pulled a carton of eggs out of a bag. "Anyone want breakfast?"

Ten

"Hey, Jared, you going to eat this sandwich or turn it into a science project?"

Jared looked up from the payroll log he was working on and stared at Slater. The foreman, his head stuck in the office refrigerator, was foraging for food.

"You just started your shift and already you're looking for something to eat?" Jared grumbled. "There's a diner in town, Slater. Try it sometime."

Shaking his head, Jared attacked the figures in front of him again. He'd been back to work eight days since the accident, but he was still trying to play catch-up, not only with his work on the well, but with the paperwork, too.

At least the operation of the rig had been running smoothly. There'd been no more problems since the compressor had blown. Jared had told Slater his suspicions, and they'd both been watching closely for anything out of the ordinary. But there'd been nothing even to raise an eyebrow over, and Jared was convinced that the problems were, in fact, coincidental and nothing more.

He'd even managed to avoid Myrna, though Jared knew that his stepmother had stopped by to "say hello" at least twice. Even Myrna knew better than to step within twenty feet of the rig when the drill was running, so if Jared saw her approaching from the main road, he conveniently found something to do up on the platform. The best way to deal with Myrna was to not deal with her at all.

A dry sandwich and a can of soda in his hands, Slater shut the refrigerator door and sat at the desk across from Jared. "I was going to eat in town, but Annie was there having dinner with that head honcho from Arloco. I thought she might like some privacy."

Privacy? Jared broke the tip of the pencil he was using and cursed silently. What the hell did she need privacy for? He frowned at the thought of Annie's having dinner with any man, but especially some snoop from Arloco. He knew she'd picked up her supervisor at the airport earlier that afternoon; he'd wanted to be at the site as they approached the target zone, which would be sometime tomorrow.

Three years of waiting. Three weeks of work. And tomorrow it would all be over. Tomorrow they would hit the depth Jonathan—and Annie—had projected for the oil trap. There was no reason to go on beyond that. Arloco would not authorize drilling any farther, so the well would have to shut down.

And Annie would go home.

He felt as if he'd been turned inside out, leaving every nerve exposed. The thought of her leaving was agony, the thought of her staying, impossible.

Slater opened the soda can and set it on the desk, then unwrapped the sandwich and sniffed at it as he propped one boot on the desk corner. "You ever get tired of being single, Jared?"

Startled by Slater's question, Jared looked up. Slater and he had never discussed bachelorhood. They'd both had their reasons for not marrying, and neither had ever questioned the other.

When Jared didn't answer, Slater continued, "I think about it occasionally. Especially when I'm forced to eat something like this."

"Nobody's forcing you to do anything," Jared said tightly. "Except get your foot off my desk."

Slater ignored him and took a bite of the sandwich. "Mornings are bad, too. I always wondered what it would be like to wake up with a soft curvy body next to mine."

Jared stared at his friend incredulously. "You're thirty-three years old, Slater. You mean to tell me you've never spent the night with a woman?"

"I never said I didn't spend the night." He pulled something green out of the sandwich and eyed it suspiciously before he popped it into his mouth. "It's the *mornings* I never seemed to stick around for."

Jared couldn't stop the image of Annie that came to mind the morning after his accident. He'd woken up, just as the sun was rising, and watched her sleep. She'd looked so peaceful, so comfortable. He'd pulled her warm body close to his and fallen back to sleep with her nestled against him. It had felt so right.

But it had been wrong.

He knew it then, as he knew it now. He was just having one hell of a time accepting that fact, even though he had managed to keep away from her since that night. It had been the most miserable week of his life.

"I think I'm going to get married," Slater announced.

Jared rolled his eyes. "Don't you think you might try dating someone first?"

"Okay." He chewed thoughtfully. "How about Annie?"

"What!"

"How about Annie? She's not hard to look at. We like each other."

Not hard to look at? Like each other? Anger simmered in Jared's stomach. He laid his pencil down and stared hard at Slater. "If I didn't think you were trying to get me going," he said carefully, "I've have to drop you flat."

"Why are you getting so mad?" Slater took another bite of sandwich.

"I'm not mad!" he yelled. "You haven't seen mad if you think this is mad!"

"What the hell are you so touchy about? You don't seem to want her, so I don't see why I can't have her."

"Have her?" Jared stood, oblivious to the fact he'd knocked Slater's soda over. "*Have* her?" It was too much. Something inside him snapped. He came around the desk and knocked Slater's foot off the desk.

"Hey!" Slater straightened. "I'm eating here. What's your problem?"

"You so much as lay one finger on Annie and you'll be eating this." He waved his fist under Slater's nose.

"You know, Jared, if I didn't know better, I might think you were jealous."

"I don't give a damn what you think!" Jared shouted. "As long as those thoughts have nothing to do with Annie!"

"What about me?"

Both men turned toward the office door. Annie stood there, a puzzled look on her face as her gaze swung from Jared to Slater and back again.

Jared felt his throat go dry. Annie was wearing a fitted long-sleeved white top that crisscrossed to a low V in the front, and a deep blue sash hugged the waistband of her long flowing blue print skirt.

She looked beautiful and sexy. Why the hell was she dressed like that for a dinner with her manager?

"What are you doing here?" he snapped.

She raised on eyebrow. "Why wouldn't I be here? I happen to work here."

Jared watched Annie's skirt swirl around her long legs as she moved into the room. He tried his damnedest not to think about those legs wrapped around his waist, but it was no good. "You're not exactly dressed for work," he said stiffly.

"Hey, Annie," Slater piped up. "You clean up real nice. You can dress like that any time, and I won't complain."

Eyes narrowed, Jared turned on Slater. The arguing started all over again.

What in the world was going on here? Annie wondered, trying to understand what it was the two men were arguing about. She'd never seen Jared and Slater get into it like this before.

That was when she spotted the overturned soda. What wasn't dripping off the side had spilled onto the desk.

"My map!" Annie cried, and rushed over to the desk. A brown fizzy puddle streaked across the map she'd been charting. "Look what you've done!"

She yanked tissues out of the desk drawer and blotted at the liquid. Like two children who'd been struggling over a toy and broken it, both men were instantly silent.

"I've been working on this for almost three weeks," she said quietly, and swallowed down the sob gathering in her throat.

"Annie, I'm sorry." Jared moved beside her and stared down at the brown stain on the map. Red, blue and orange lines ran together. "It was my fault."

Slater stood and stuck his hands in his pockets. "Yeah. Me, too, Annie. But it really was my fault."

"No." Jared shook his head. "I was taking my bad mood out on Slater."

"I started it," Slater disagreed.

They started to argue then over whose fault it was.

"Stop it!" Annie slammed her hand down on the desk. "I don't give a damn whose fault it is."

She felt tears burn her eyes. The men fell silent again. She stared down at the map and thought of all the hours she'd put into recharting it. Frustration built in her. Frustration that she'd never found what she was looking for, even though she knew it was there. Staring her right in the face.

And now she'd never have a chance to find it.

That seemed to be the way her entire life was going.

Muttering under her breath, she did her best to salvage the map. It would have to go into the file when she got back to Dallas and gave her report. At least she'd have *something* to show for all her work.

"How'd your meeting go?" Jared asked tentatively.

"Fine," she said tersely. "I told Ken we should hit the zone late in the afternoon. He'll come by sometime before that."

He nodded slowly, and Annie felt her anger melt away when she saw the strain etched in Jared's eyes. Every moment had been building toward tomorrow, and she knew how much it meant to him.

"Jared," she said, letting out a long breath, "why don't you go home? I know you've been working since before the sun came up, and tomorrow is going to be a long day, too.''

Annie couldn't identify the look in Jared's eyes as he stared at her, but it made her skin flush with heat and her insides ache with longing. His gaze slid slowly over her, as if he was memorizing every inch of her.

''She's right.'' Slater ran a hand through his thick brown hair, then picked up his hard hat and settled it on his head. ''Go on home and get some rest. I can keep Annie company.'' He looked at Annie and winked.

Keep her company? Why did anyone need to keep her company? There was a tone in Slater's voice that Annie had never heard before. She frowned at the man.

Something was going on between these two that involved her, Annie realized. Something she didn't think she was going to like one little bit.

''You trying to get rid of me?'' Jared stared at Slater.

Slater raised one brow innocently. ''Why would I want to do that?''

Annie groaned as it started up again between them. Jared's face was red with anger as he leaned in close and yelled at Slater. And Slater, a half smile on his face, was obviously egging his friend on.

Macho idiots. She stepped between them and put one hand on each of their chests. She tried to push them apart, but it was like standing between two steel beams set in concrete. ''What the hell is going on between you two?''

A muscle jumped in Jared's temple. ''Nothing.''

Slater just grinned.

''We've only got one more day of drilling, boys,'' Annie said with exasperation. ''Then you two can go at it. At least I won't be around to have to watch.''

Annie felt the shift of tension in Jared's body as he pulled his gaze from Slater and looked at her. They'd never discussed her leaving, though they both knew she'd be going back to Dallas when the project was through.

Since his accident, he'd been careful not to touch her or even be alone with her. But she'd caught him watching her when he thought she didn't see, and the look in his eyes had been so hungry it had taken her breath away.

She'd hoped, even prayed, that he would ask her to stay. That he'd be able to let go of the past and start over. With her.

But he hadn't. And as each day passed, and the target zone came closer, she knew he never would.

She dropped her hands and stepped away, no longer caring whether or not they beat each other to a pulp. In fact, she decided, she just might enjoy it if they did.

She turned her back on the men. "And since I no longer have a map to work on, I'll just clear out my things now, instead of tomorrow."

What was the point in waiting until tomorrow, anyway? she thought, opening the top drawer where she'd kept her pencils and pens and other miscellaneous items. It would only be that much more difficult. Better just to get it done, and then she could leave here and never look back. She could forget about Jared and how much her heart was breaking.

And while she was at it she could also stop the sun from rising and predict earthquakes.

"Annie..." Jared made a move toward her, but when their eyes met, his jaw tightened, and he turned away. "I'll see you in the morning."

"Fine." A tightness closed around Annie's chest as she watched Jared leave. *Damn you, Jared Stone.*

She sighed heavily and sat at the desk, then looked at Slater. "You want to tell me what that was all about?"

Slater sat on the edge of the desk and tipped back his hat. "What's the expression? 'You can run, but you can't hide.' He's just about run out of hiding places, and it's making him mad as hell. That, and the way he feels about you."

She laughed dryly. "Oh, you mean how he can't wait until I'm gone?"

"No, Bailey, that's not what I mean." He looked at her for a long time, as if searching for the right words. "You really don't know, do you?"

She ran a finger over the blurred lines of the map. "Know what?"

"Jared's in love with you. He has been since the first day he laid eyes on you."

Slowly, deliberately, she lifted her gaze to Slater's. "I don't know what you're talking about."

One corner of Slater's mouth lifted. "I think you do."

"No." She shook her head. "He's done everything to keep as far away from me as possible since the day I came back."

"I'm not just talking about now," Slater said as he held her gaze. "I'm talking about from the first time he met you. When Jonathan brought you home. He's been in love with you from day one."

She went perfectly still. All she could do was stare at Slater. It couldn't be. *It couldn't be.* Jared? In love with her? Back then? She'd have known, she'd have seen *something*.

Wouldn't she?

"That's not possible," she whispered.

"He wasn't any happier about it then than he is now, but it's true, all right."

"How—" she drew in a breath to steady herself "—how could you know? Jared never would have told you that."

"Whiskey does a lot of things to a man, Bailey. Makes him forget, and it also loosens his tongue. We drank a lot of whiskey in Venezuela."

Something flickered in Slater's eyes, a remembrance of a time past, but it was gone before Annie could identify it. "But he wouldn't have had to tell me," Slater said. "It's written in fluorescent letters all over his face. He loves you, all right."

Because her head was spinning, she closed her eyes. "Why... why are you telling me this?"

"Because Jared's too bullheaded to. And that's what this is all about, Bailey. It's about a second chance. A time to make things right, to put the past to rest and move on."

"But he never let on. He never even looked at me."

"Of course not," Slater said. "There was a special bond between Jared and Jonathan, something only twins completely understand. You knocked Jared out cold the first time he saw you. He hated himself because he wanted you to be his. He's never forgiven himself for it."

"And then Jonathan died," she said quietly.

Slater nodded. "He felt that he'd betrayed Jonathan by falling in love with you. When Jared couldn't save Jonathan the night he fell, it only added to the guilt he was already feeling. If I hadn't been behind Jared and held him back, I swear he'd have jumped off the rig after Jonathan."

Annie closed her eyes and folded her arms tightly to her, trying to stop the image of Jared having to watch his brother die, the feeling of helplessness....

Slater pulled her from the chair and put his big arms around her. When her shaking finally eased, she pulled away and looked at him. "Tonight, when I came in—you and Jared were arguing about me, weren't you?"

Slater grinned. "I told Jared I wanted to marry you."

"You did what?" She backed away and put her hands on her hips.

"Well, I told Jared I was going to take you out on a date first."

She frowned at him. "How thoughtful of you."

Slater's grin broadened. "Jared didn't think so. He wanted to punch me out."

She folded her arms. "So he won't have me, and he doesn't think anyone else should, either."

"Something like that."

An unreasonable anger built in her. Anger and frustration. Disappointment. Pain. All of it coursed through her. Hadn't she had enough?

Yes.

It was time to fight back. She narrowed her eyes and strode purposefully to the door.

"Hey, Bailey."

She stopped at the doorway and looked over her shoulder at Slater.

"I would, you know."

"Would what?"

"Marry you."

She walked back to him, then touched his cheek and kissed him lightly on the lips. "Thanks, Slater," she said softly. "If I thought you were serious, I might take you up on it."

He smiled, and she thought he'd never looked so handsome.

Then, squaring her shoulders, she turned and left the office, determined to have it out with Jared once and for all.

Jared kicked the front door shut behind him and stalked into the kitchen. He stared long and hard at the bottle of whiskey on the counter, then swore and pulled a beer out of the refrigerator, instead.

Bottle in hand, he rummaged through the cupboards for something to eat. Cans and boxes stared coldly back at him. He slammed the doors and swore again.

Hey, Jared, you ever get tired of being single?

Slater's voice echoed in his head. Jared knew that his friend had been messing with him, but he'd been in no mood for it. In fact, he'd been looking for a way to relieve some of the tension that had been building in him as the target date came closer. Even if Slater hadn't been serious, punching the man in the face would have gone far toward alleviating that stress.

But what if Slater *had* been serious? Jared scowled at the bottle in his hand. What if he'd meant it when he said he wanted to marry Annie?

Nah. Jared shook his head. Slater had been hassling him, that's all. He wasn't the marrying kind.

Was he?

Jared remembered the way Annie had looked in that skirt and tight-fitting top. Just a glance from that woman could bring the strongest man to his knees.

He started to raise the bottle of beer to his mouth, then banged it down on the counter. Dammit, anyway! Why had he left them alone together like that? He started to head for the front door, then stopped.

One more day. He only had to get through one more day. Whether they hit oil or not, Annie would be leaving. He'd have to learn to live with that.

He started to turn away when the front door flew open, and the object of his attention stood in the doorway. She slammed the door behind her and marched up to him.

"Jared Stone—" she leveled her gaze with his "—do you love me?"

Shocked, he stared at her. "What?"

"I said, do you love me?"

He couldn't be hearing her right. But she'd asked him twice. *Do you love me?* Panic gripped him. How could he answer that. He *couldn't* answer that.

"Annie," he choked out. "I can't . . . you can't . . ."

"Can't what?" She moved closer.

He could feel the sweat bead his brow. He wanted to back away, to turn and run, but his feet felt like lead. "For God's sake . . ."

"The truth. That's all I'm asking for. Just say it, Jared."

Heart pounding, he stared down at her. Her cheeks were flushed, her hazel eyes intense. She stood so close he could smell the floral perfume she wore, feel the heat of her body. His fingers curled, his palms ached, he wanted her so bad.

Do you love me? He never allowed himself to think the words, let alone say them out loud. Well, except for one time, in a moment of weakness. The only person who'd ever known, the only person he'd ever told was . . .

Slater.

It was like a kick in the stomach. He went very still. "What did Slater tell you?"

She didn't blink an eye. "That you fell in love with me the first time we met."

He was going to kill his foreman. Slowly. Painfully. "Slater has a big mouth."

"He's honest, which is more than I can say for you. Maybe it wouldn't be such a bad idea for me to marry him."

Jared clenched his teeth. "Did he ask you?"

"In a way."

"What did you say?" His voice was iron hard.

"I told him I'd think about it."

He decided he wouldn't kill the man. He'd torture him. That would be more satisfying. "You don't love him."

"So what? The man I do love is too big a jackass to even tell me he loves me. Why should I waste my time?"

The room was growing smaller, the corners moving in on him. He said nothing, just stood there, feeling as if a steel band was closing around his chest. He saw the pain and disappointment in her eyes.

"Goodbye, Jared," she said softly, and turned away.

Without thinking, he took hold of her shoulders and brought her back around to face him. "Look at me, Annie," he said raggedly.

She kept her gaze on the floor.

"Annie, please, *look at me.*"

Jaw set, she complied. Her eyes were bright with unshed tears.

"I can't love you."

She flinched at his words. "Because of me, or because of Jonathan?"

"Don't do this to me—"

"To you! Don't do this to *you?*" She jerked out of his hold. "You are one self-centered bastard, Jared Stone. You're so wrapped up in your own guilt, have you once thought about *me?* About what I'm feeling?"

She tried to leave, but he grabbed her again. She struggled, but he held on to her tightly, forcing her to look at him.

"*Thought* about you?" he said with a hoarse laugh. "Lady, there isn't a moment goes by I don't think about you. Not one minute I don't wish to God that things were different, that I didn't love you so much my insides ache from wanting you."

He closed his eyes, realizing he'd said it. He'd told her he loved her. Annie stilled in his arms. When he opened his eyes again, he saw a tear slide down her cheek.

"I do love you, Annie," he said again, and pulled her tightly to him. "I love you so much it scares the hell out of me."

He brought his mouth to hers. It was impossible not to. He tasted the salt of her tears, felt the quiet sob from her throat as he deepened the kiss. Her arms slid around his neck and he lifted her off the floor, grinding his mouth against hers like a man obsessed.

She clung to him, whimpering, and he carried her to the bedroom. His lips never left hers as he let her body slide down his until her feet touched the floor. She was so soft, so precious. He'd never wanted like this before; he never would again. She was the only woman he'd ever loved, and the realization was so profound he could hardly breathe.

He would have stopped, pulled away before this went any further, but she wrapped her arms tightly around his neck and lifted her body snugly against his, moving against him in a way that drove all rational thought from his mind. There was only Annie and the wild driving need pumping through his body to possess her in the most primitive way.

He tugged at the sash of her skirt, pulling it loose, then dropping it to the floor. Impatient with the barrier of clothes between them, he quickly pulled her blouse away from her shoulders, unhooked her lacy white bra and slid both articles of clothing off, letting them fall beside the sash. He cupped her breasts and caressed the hardened tips, then bent her backward, giving him the freedom to taste the sweetness of her soft skin. She arched her back, straining against him as he took her into his mouth, murmuring her pleasure.

Annie was on fire from Jared's touch. Her breasts felt full and tight, and every touch and stroke of Jared's tongue sent sparks of pleasure racing over her skin. She burrowed her hands into his hair, murmuring incoherently to him.

I love you. His words careened through her, making her dizzy with elation. She was in a whirlwind of sensation, certain she would be swept away at any moment, terrified that it was a dream and she would wake up. But he'd said it. *I love you.* She knew that didn't make him like it, but it was a start.

"Jared," she whispered, "I love you."

He moaned, and she wasn't sure if it was desire or despair, but she knew that she loved him so much she thought her heart might burst. The light of the setting sun was like a haze in the room, settling over their bodies in a soft golden glow.

"Make love to me, Jared," she murmured. "Please."

"I am, sweetheart. I am."

He gathered the fabric of her skirt in his hands and lifted it, then slid his hand over her hip. He watched her, his eyes dark with passion as he pressed his knee between hers, opening her legs wider as he moved his hand over the smooth skin of her inner thighs. His fingers moved upward and traced the thin strip of her lace underwear. She shuddered at his touch.

There was a freedom in their lovemaking that hadn't been there before, an openness and honesty that had been missing the first time. It made the pleasure more intense, more exciting, and she reveled in the feeling, torn between wanting to laugh or cry at the depth of emotion swirling through her. She slid her hands up his arms and gripped his shoulders, holding on tightly because she was sure her knees would not be able to hold her.

He couldn't take his eyes off her. Her lips, still wet and swollen from his kiss, were parted, and her eyes were heavy with desire. Desire for him. *For him.* The realization surged through him like a thunderbolt. He cupped the silky juncture of her legs in his palm, marveling at the texture of her soft skin against his callused hand. She sighed when he slid one finger under the top band of lace, then gasped when he dipped lower and lightly stroked the sensitive folds of velvety flesh.

His heart pounded frantically in his chest. His blood raced as he delved into the liquid heat of her body. She was so tight, so ready for him. An urgency gripped him, and he pulled her closer, hungrily covering her mouth with his as he continued to caress her.

And then she was as crazy as he was. She twisted away from him, as if the pleasure was more than she could bear. She struggled with the buttons of his shirt, releasing them one by one, moving her hands and mouth over his bare chest, exploring every hard angle, making his skin burn, turning his insides into an inferno of need. He moaned when her hand moved lower to unsnap his jeans, then sucked in a sharp breath when she slid denim and underwear smoothly down his hips, freeing him for her touch.

Deep ragged breaths consumed him as he closed his eyes, luxuriating in the sensation of her smooth fingers stroking him. It wasn't possible to feel this intensely, this desperately, he thought, moving his hands over her shoulders and back. It couldn't be possible. He'd heard a man could die from this kind of pleasure, but he'd never believed it. Now he wasn't so sure.

They fell to the bed, and the mattress sank beneath them as he covered her body with his. His mouth moved over hers as he kicked off his jeans and boots. She lifted her hips as he tugged her skirt and underwear off.

The tension building inside Annie had become unbearable. Gasping, she wrapped her arms and legs around Jared, wanting frantically to join their bodies and feel him inside her. She made a soft cry of protest when he suddenly pulled away.

Confused, she watched as he reached into the nightstand, then smiled when she saw the small silver packet he pulled out.

She wanted to help, but with her hands shaking the way they were, she was afraid she'd only delay the process, and every second he was away from her was agony.

He moved between her legs then and spread them. Once again their eyes met and held as he lowered himself. She opened her body, her heart and her soul, and pulled him tightly to her, arching her body to meet every strong thrust. The crescendo rose and built, lifting them higher and closer. Her fingers dug into his shoulders, and she cried out his name as her release burst forth in a kaleidoscope of intense sensation. He groaned, then surged hard and deep as his own climax shuddered through him.

Eleven

She lay on her side, one arm draped over the edge of the bed. Jared lay behind her, his arm circling her waist possessively. Their breathing had calmed, and the night settled over them like a satin blanket.

With a sigh, she nestled back, closer to the heat of Jared's body. He kissed her shoulder, and she smiled at the thrill that rippled through her.

"May I ask why you happened to be so, uh, prepared, Mr. Stone?" she asked teasingly.

"Well—" he nipped at the nape of her neck "—we can thank Jessica for that. She included them in the emergency bag she made up for me. I seem to recall she referred to them as 'necessities.'"

"*Jessica* bought them for you—because of me?" Annie groaned and buried her face in the pillow. "How can I ever face her again?"

Jared chuckled, and she felt the rush of air against her neck. "She's a big girl, Annie. No doubt she suspected something was up between us and—"

They both burst out laughing at his choice of words. Jessica more than suspected, Annie thought, recalling her lunch with his sister. Jared didn't need to know that, though.

Turning to face him, she pressed her mouth to his jaw, and his beard bristled her lips. The sensation sent a shiver through her. "Well, then, I suppose I'll just have to thank her."

"Annie," he said quietly, and she already decided she didn't like the tone, "you never told me. Do you know yet about..."

She shook her head. "It'll be a few more days."

They were silent then, neither one of them certain what to say. She didn't tell him that she'd bought a home-pregnancy test, but hadn't had the courage to use it. She'd wanted to wait until she got back to Dallas, where she could deal with the results, whatever they were, by herself. She didn't want Jared to be with her because of any responsibility he might feel toward her, but because he loved her and could finally put the past behind them.

At least they'd overcome one of those obstacles, she thought with a smile. He *did* love her, though getting him to admit it had been like cutting a tree down with a pocket knife. Letting go of the past for Jared was going to be doubly hard.

And as much as she wasn't ready to face the issue at this moment, it wasn't going to get any easier by putting it off.

"Jared," she said gently, "we have to talk about it."

She felt his body tense beside hers. "About what?"

"About what Slater told me."

He sat up and reached across her to turn on the light. For one terrible moment she thought he was going to leave. Instead, he propped his elbows on his knees and raked his hands through his hair.

"Do you remember the first day Jonathan brought you to Stone Creek?"

She pulled the sheet around her and sat up, brushing his shoulder with hers. "You were on the rig, tightening one of the drill pipes, I think."

He nodded. "Did you ever wonder why he brought you to the rig first, instead of the house?"

Now that she thought about it, Jonathan *had* driven right past Stone Creek Ranch and gone to the rig. "I never thought about it."

"He brought you here first because he wanted you to meet me before the rest of the family. Not because he needed my approval, but because he wanted to know I liked you."

He gave a dry laugh and curled his hands tightly in his hair. "I liked you all right. The minute you stepped out of that car and smiled at me, I felt as if I'd been poleaxed."

His words stunned her. She closed her eyes, trying to remember something about that day. "You barely looked at me," she said softly. "You were busy working and said you were too dirty to shake my hand."

"It was my mind that was dirty." He shook his head in disgust. "My own brother, my twin, brings his fiancée to meet me, and I'm having fantasies about her the moment we meet. It made me sick to my stomach."

Annie sighed heavily. "Jared, it doesn't matter now. And Jonathan never knew."

He turned toward her and took her by the shoulders. "*I* knew, Annie. I should have stopped it right then and there. Pushed every thought of you out of my mind."

Her chest ached at the torment she heard in his voice. "You would have, Jared. If Jonathan had lived, you would have."

"No." He shook his head. "Even all these years made no difference. I couldn't control what I felt for you then, just as I can't now. If Jonathan had lived, I'd still want you. I'd still love you."

It was strange how those words brought such joy and such sorrow at the same time. She'd wanted desperately to hear them, but seeing the misery they gave Jared only tightened the ache in her chest. How was she going to make him understand he'd done nothing wrong? That there were some things that went beyond control, some things that a person was powerless to prevent?

"We both loved Jonathan. Neither one of us would have ever hurt him. He knew that." She reached up and gently touched Jared's cheek. "But Jonathan loved us, too. I don't believe for one second that he wouldn't want us to be together now."

As if in pain, Jared closed his eyes. "I have this dream," he said hoarsely. "It's the same one over and over. I'm with you, like this, and Jonathan walks in. He accuses me of betraying him. Of stealing you from him. Then he wants to know why I didn't save him, why I didn't stop him from falling." Jared opened his eyes and Annie saw the anguish there. "I wake up then, in a sweat asking myself the same question."

She was crying now, and though he stiffened when she circled his waist with her arms, he didn't pull away. "That's not Jonathan," she said through the thickness in her throat. "That's you. You couldn't have stopped Jonathan, or you would have. I know it, Jonathan knows it, and in your heart, you know it, too. You would have traded places with him up there on that rig, and still would, if it were possible."

She lifted her face and looked at him. "But it's not possible, Jared. *It's not possible.*"

He stared at her, but she had no idea if he really heard her. "I think I see him sometimes," he said distantly. "The back of his head in a crowd. Or through the window of the Cactus Flat café, sitting at a table, reading a paper."

His shoulders sagged as he let out a long breath. "Once, early in the morning, I even thought I saw him up on the rig. He was smiling. Then he just disappeared, and I knew I'd been imagining it, seeing what I wanted to see."

"Maybe not, Jared," Annie whispered. "Maybe that was his way of saying goodbye to you."

She felt him tremble, then wrap his arms around her and pull her close. She held him tightly, terrified that this was Jared's way of saying goodbye to her.

She refused to think about that now. Whether she left or she stayed, at least they'd been honest with other. He knew she loved him, and she knew he loved her.

But if that would be enough for Jared to let go of the past, she still didn't know.

As they neared the target zone of 12,360 feet, the tension on the rig was stretched taut. Every crew member knew how critical the final feet of drilling were, and as the time approached, a silence closed around the site. The men's faces were somber, and there was none of the usual conversation or joking that lightened the otherwise tedious hard work. Even Slater, who was always calm, seemed anxious as he stood to the side with Ken, Annie's supervisor, and explained the operation.

The drill man called out a depth of 12,340 feet.

Jared had felt pressure on every rig he'd worked on, but nothing as oppressive as this. He knew that every man here was pulling for him; they wanted to hit oil almost as badly as he did. They'd been a good crew, a loyal crew, even sticking around through the permit fiasco. He wanted to give them a bonus, but unless they hit pay dirt today—within the next half hour—they'd all be standing in the unemployment line together.

And with no way to pay back the mortgage he'd taken out on the land, he'd lose his parcel of Stone Creek completely.

One month ago, that thought had been inconceivable. Now—he glanced at Annie—he knew that wasn't the worst thing that could happen.

He watched her as she knelt in the wet slushy dirt, her clothes covered with mud as she pulled up core samples from the drilling pipes and examined them. Between the seismics and the meticulous mapping, they knew almost to the foot where the trap might be. If they hit oil, the samples would clearly show the slimy black gold. There'd be no dramatic burst or gush of oil as depicted in the movies, just a simple inspection of the dirt being brought up. If they didn't hit it, it was Annie's responsibility as Arloco's geologist to shut the operation down.

There'd be no reason to proceed beyond what was mapped. Arloco wouldn't approve it, and it would be Annie's head if she went more than ten feet beyond what was authorized.

12,350 feet.

Because there was nothing else he could do at this point, and because he knew she was too busy to notice, he allowed himself the luxury of watching her. There wasn't much to see actually. A blanket of mud enclosed her long sleek body, a hard hat covered her silky blond hair, and the goggles she wore hid most of her face. And still, she was the most beautiful woman he'd ever seen.

God, how he wanted her. He wanted to watch those lips curve into a smile that could brighten the darkest room; he wanted to hear that soft sexy voice that could bring a man to his knees or cut him to ribbons. Most of all, he wanted her here, with him. In his bed, in his life.

He wanted too much.

His stomach twisted as he forced himself to look away from her. He didn't want to think about how wonderful it had felt to go to sleep, and wake up, with her in his arms. Not now, not when she'd be leaving in a few hours. He'd never make it through the day if he tortured himself that way.

Their conversation this morning had been more like that of polite strangers than lovers. They'd dressed quietly, and when she'd stood at the front door, her hand on the knob, and softly said goodbye, he'd heard the finality in her voice. It had taken every ounce of willpower he possessed not to drag her back.

But he couldn't. No matter how much he loved her, Jonathan would always be there between them. Annie deserved better than that. She deserved a man who would love her without reserve, without guilt. And that man wasn't him.

"Jared!"

He turned at the sound of his name, then swore silently as he watched Myrna and her father walk toward him.

Not now. Of all the times he didn't want to deal with his stepmother, this certainly had to be at the top of the list.

"We thought we'd stop by and see how it's going."

Convenient timing, Jared thought sourly. If Annie didn't find oil in the next few minutes, Myrna would be the first to know he'd failed. Vultures moved in fast. No doubt she already had a check written to buy his part of Stone Creek.

There was also no doubt he'd tell her what she could do with that check.

"I hear today is the day." Carlton extended his hand to Jared. "Just wanted to wish you good luck."

"Thanks." Jared shook the man's hand and noted how pale he was. Carlton Hewitt had always been a tenacious corporate man who was known for his aggressive business dealings. It seemed strange to see the man finally beginning to show his age.

"Why don't you go help yourself to something cold to drink in the fridge?" Jared offered, gesturing toward the office. If he couldn't get rid of them, at least he wouldn't have to look at them.

"Thanks, son." Carlton slapped Jared's back. "Don't mind if we do."

Frowning, Jared watched Myrna and her father disappear into the office, then turned his attention back to the rig.

12,360 feet.

Now or never. They'd go ten feet beyond the target zone, then stop.

For the next few minutes, he went through the motions of checking on the equipment and talking to the men, but with each sweep of the second hand on his watch, he felt the band around his chest pull tighter and tighter.

12,370 feet.

He watched as Annie slowly straightened. She stood there for a long moment, staring at the sample in her hand, then removed her hat and goggles and looked up at Jared.

Jaw set, he walked over to her.

Her gaze held his, then she shook her head.

He knew he should feel something. Anger. Frustration. Disappointment. But the fact was, he felt nothing.

Absolutely nothing.

"Jared—"

He raised a hand and cut her off, then turned toward Slater. "Shut the drills down."

Slater glanced at Annie, his dark eyes narrowed. She nodded slowly.

Slater whistled to the drill man and sliced a hand through the air. The engines slowed, stopped, then the compressor was shut down, too.

The sound of quiet was deafening. No one spoke. No one moved.

Jared drew air into a chest that felt hollow and faced the crew. Their expressions were grave as they watched him. "I want to thank you all for working for me. I'm sorry it was a bust, but I appreciate your hanging in there with me when it got sticky. You've been a good crew."

Glenn, who'd been standing next to Annie, took his hat off and stepped forward. "What are you going to do now, boss?"

It was the same question on Annie's mind. The mud covering her body suddenly felt like lead, and she couldn't have moved her feet if she'd tried. There was nothing more she could do, nothing anyone could do, and the realization that it was over pierced her heart.

What are *you going to do, Jared?* she asked silently.

Jared's eyes met hers for the briefest of moments, then flicked away. "There's a call out for a rig in Venezuela. Anyone interested in a little foreign travel, let me know. In the meantime, you can settle up your pay with Slater."

An emptiness settled over Annie. *He was leaving.* Just like that. She hadn't really thought he would, not with Jessica and Jake and Emma here. She knew how much his family meant to him. And deep in her heart, she'd even hoped that he might want to stay for her, because he did love her, and maybe, just maybe, they might have a chance.

Jared turned to her then, his eyes hollow as he looked down at her. "Thank you, Annie," he said without emotion. "In spite of what you might think, I'm glad you were here. I'm sorry this didn't work out."

She watched in amazement as he started for the office, but when he saw Myrna and Carlton standing in the doorway, he turned sharply and headed for his truck.

Thank you? Sorry this didn't work out?

That was how he said goodbye?

So much for second chances, she thought, curling her hands into fists.

Cold anger suddenly filled the vacuum inside her. She was tired of trying to understand his hurt and guilt. Tired of her own hurt. She'd loved Jonathan, and when he'd died, she'd thought her world had fallen apart. But time had slowly put it back together and eased the pain. She'd been fortunate to find love again, a deeper stronger love that came with a maturity she hadn't had the first time. And now she'd lost that, too.

It made her mad as hell.

She followed him to the truck, her boots throwing mud with every angry step. He'd already started the engine when she appeared beside him, her eyes narrowed.

"Annie, I'm sorry, I—"

"Save it," she snapped. "I don't want to hear it. You're a damn fool, Jared Stone. You can run as far as you want, but someday you're going to run out of places to hide," she said, repeating Slater's words. "Then what will you do?"

She turned and walked away before he could respond, and when his truck drove off, she swallowed the thick knot in her throat. All she wanted to do was get the rest of her things and get out of here. She headed for the office, cringing at the thought of having to deal with Myrna right now. At least Carlton had gone outside and was talking to a couple of the crew members.

Myrna was sitting behind the desk, using the phone, but quickly hung up when Annie walked in. She stood and bestowed her with a pitying look. "Oh, Annie, you must feel so awful. And Jared, the poor dear," she went on. "He looked so devastated."

"Mrs. Stone, please excuse me," Annie said coolly, "but I have some work to finish up in here."

"Why, yes, of course. I'll just get out of your way." Myrna picked up her purse and started for the door. "Don't be too hard on yourself, dear. It's not your fault."

Holding back the sigh of exasperation in her throat, Annie just shook her head as the woman left the office, then sat at the desk. The map that Jared and Slater had spilled soda on was still spread out on the desktop.

It's not your fault.

Annie froze as Myrna's words sank in.

A strange sensation came over her, a feeling as if she'd suddenly remembered something she'd forgotten long ago.

It's not your fault.

The dark stain on the map stared at her. The image of Jared and Slater arguing about it sprang into her mind. Frowning, she closed her eyes and concentrated.

It's my fault, Jared had said.

No, it's my fault, Slater disagreed.

But it was *both* their faults.

Two faults!

With a gasp, her eyes flew open. There were two faults! That was what had been staring at her all these weeks. Two faults with oil traps. But she'd been so busy fine-tuning the first fault, wanting to make sure she had it exact, that she'd neglected to look for another.

The logs and seismics would prove her theory, but she hadn't much time. It could be another ten feet, or another hundred. But it was there. She knew it. She didn't know how she knew it, but she did.

She ran to the office door. She searched frantically for Slater and found him standing by the compressor, preparing to release the air from the hoses.

"Slater!" He turned, his brows raised as she ran at him, waving her arms. "Wait! We're not done yet."

Myrna and Carlton were getting into their car, but stopped at Annie's announcement. The men, who'd been milling around to talk, looked over.

"Slater." She stopped in front of the foreman and grabbed him by the arms. "Get the crew back in place. There's a second fault. I'll need a little time to map an approximate, but I know it's there."

Slater frowned at her. "You can't do that, Bailey. Arloco will can you if we drill beyond what's authorized."

"Where's Ken?" she asked, searching the area for her her supervisor. "I'll get him to okay it."

Slater shook his head. "He already left. Said to tell you he'd see you back in Dallas."

No! Ken was the only one who could approve an extension. And she wouldn't be able to reach him now for hours. *Dammit.* She couldn't give up.

She *wouldn't.*

"Let them can me. I don't care. I'll take full responsibility. It won't come back at you."

"You think I'd give a damn if it did?" He gave her a long, searching look then nodded slowly. "All right, Bailey, you're the boss."

From the corner of her eye, Annie saw Myrna and Carlton approaching. She leaned in close to Slater and whispered, "See if you can keep the dogs chained, okay? I need some quiet."

Slater's smile was devilish. "No problem."

Ignoring Myrna, Annie hurried back into the office. She heard Myrna call her, but quickly slammed the office door shut and locked it.

Annie closed her eyes and said a silent prayer. She drew in a deep breath to calm herself and cleared everything from her mind. She couldn't let Myrna or Arloco, or even Jared, interfere with her now.

He stood under the oak tree and stared up at the wide spreading branches. A warm wind softly rustled the leaves, and the low-pitched chirp of a resident bird carried on the breeze. Autumn touched the late-afternoon air.

Jared had climbed this tree many times as a child. He and Jonathan had chiseled their names in the coarse bark. He moved to that spot, surprised at how far down he had to look to find the carvings. Twenty-two years ago, they'd been eye level.

He knelt and touched his fingers to the roughened edges of his brother's name. It was still clear, though weathered with time. Jonathan had cut his thumb with his pocket knife that day and insisted Jared cut his, too, so they could be blood brothers. Jared remembered arguing the issue, saying they were already blood brothers, and there was no point in both of them bleeding. The argument degenerated into name-calling, then fists flying. When Jared's nose started to bleed, Jonathan got his way.

The smile on Jared's face slowly faded. Who'd have thought that at age twenty-nine one of them would be buried under this tree in the family cemetery.

He drew in a slow breath and moved to the first headstone, paying his respects to his mother first.

Helen Roberta Stone, Beloved Wife and Mother. Images flashed through his mind. Her brilliant smile as she lit birthday candles... her gray eyes narrowed with a reprimand... her soft laugh at the dinner table....

She'd been the quiet voice of reason in a house full of hotheaded impulsive men—not to mention Jessica, with her determined disposition. His father had cherished Helen, her children adored her. Her death had devastated them all, but none more than J.T. and Jessica.

He moved to his father. *Jeremiah Tobias Stone.* The image in his mind now was hard piercing blue eyes. He'd been a strong hardworking man who showed his love with a look or touch, but never with words. And even though they'd argued when he'd closed down the well, Jared knew his father had done it because he loved him.

Jared still remembered the night before he'd left for South America. J.T. had stood at the door, watching his son pack. "Just remember, son," J.T. had said, "no matter where you go or what you do, your family will always be there for you. Always."

"I'm sorry I wasn't there for you, Dad," Jared said softly now.

He stepped to the final grave and stared unblinking at the dry earth, then at the simple block of granite.

Jonathan Graham Stone.

He'd gone from a name carved on a tree to a name carved in a headstone.

A heavy ache grew in Jared's chest, moving upward, closing his throat and blinding his eyes.

"We didn't hit oil, Jonathan," Jared said. "All those plans, all the years of preparing. Nothing. You died for *nothing*."

A feeling darker and blacker than he'd ever felt before swelled inside him. Fists clenched, he sank to his knees.

"Damn you, Jonathan Stone." Jared hit the ground with his fists. "Why weren't you here with me for this? All those years of planning, of hard work. We were supposed to do this *together*. Damn you. *Damn you*."

The wind picked up, shuddering the branches overhead. The bird flew off, chattering loudly. Jared drew in a choking breath, watching as the leaves swirled around his knees. What the hell was wrong with him, he thought, shouting at Jonathan like that? He certainly couldn't hear him. Jared looked up, listening to the whisper of the wind.

Or could he?

Slowly Jared unclenched his fists and stared at his hands. All these years he'd held a tight knot of anger inside him. Anger at himself for letting Jonathan die. For loving Annie. For going to South America. He'd worn that anger like a suit of armor, and it had shielded him from the truth. The truth of his real feeling, his true anger.

But it wasn't himself he was mad at. It was Jonathan. For dying. For leaving him behind. *How could he do that to him? They were blood brothers.*

The sound of their voices from that day came back to him: the childish laughter, the heated argument. He glanced up at the tree, and a sudden calm overcame him.

He felt no shame in the moisture on his cheeks. Only relief. He stared at the leaves gathered around his knees, felt the wind on his face and knew that Jonathan would never truly die. He would always be with him.

And as he looked at the headstone, he heard the quiet sound of goodbye.

He stood slowly and thought of a beautiful blonde with hazel-green eyes who had captured his heart the moment he'd laid eyes on her. He'd been lost.

But she'd belonged to Jonathan. And that would always be there between them. He didn't want to be second. He couldn't live with wondering if it might be Jonathan she thought of when he held her, if Jonathan's name might slip from her lips when he made love to her.

He knew he had to let her go. She deserved so much more than he could give. A man who could love without doubts, without fear. If she stayed, it would drive them apart, then drive her away. And losing her like that would be a death more torturous than anything else he could imagine.

He sighed wearily, wondering if she'd left the rig yet. He at least owed her a decent goodbye. An ache spread through his chest as the image of Annie's soft smile came to his mind. He'd loved her from the first; he would always love her.

His feet felt like lead as he walked to the truck. He drove back to the site in a daze. When he saw her Cherokee parked in front of the office, the pain in his chest tightened. She was probably still packing a few things.

He pulled in front of the office and cut the engine, then suddenly realized that the drills were running again.

"What the . . . ?"

Frowning, he glanced first at the rig, then at the office. Those drills should have been shut down more than an hour ago. What was going on?

And as he opened the truck door to go find out, the office exploded, then burst into flames.

Twelve

The blast threw him to his knees, but he was up and running before the shock wave passed.

"Annie!"

He screamed her name as he reached the blown-out front door. Flames shot through the opening. *"Annie!"*

He ducked, intending to jump through the fire, but suddenly found himself yanked backward into the dirt by a strong pair of arms. Slater was on top of him, struggling to keep him down.

"Annie!" Jared yelled. "I've got to get Annie!"

He fought like a crazy man, oblivious to what Slater was saying to him. He nearly broke loose of the huge man's hold, but several others joined in and succeeded in pinning him to the ground.

He called Annie's name over and over and thrashed wildly, determined to break loose if even a hundred men held him.

"Jared! Stop it. I'm right here. I'm fine."

Annie. It *was* Annie. She stared down at him, her brow twisted in worry. But she was fine. *Thank God, thank God...*

The men released him then and hurried off to fight the fire. Thick black smoke billowed from the burning office. Coughing, Jared staggered to his feet and dragged Annie away. Fire hoses came from two directions, and water quickly drowned the crackling flames, turning the smoke pale gray.

Jared took hold of Annie's arms and looked at her. "I—I thought you were in the office."

She shook her head. "I was up on the rig."

He looked at the office. The fire was almost out now, but a few of the men were still dousing the structure with water. Slater shouted a few orders, then turned and walked over to Annie and Jared.

"Is everyone all right?" Jared asked.

Slater nodded, his jaw set tight. "There was no one in the office or close enough to be hurt. Though I do think your stepmother screamed loud enough to break a few eardrums."

Jared glanced over and saw Myrna standing beside her car, looking pale and shaken. Carlton sat on the front seat, with the door open and his feet outside. Jared had no idea why they were still here, nor did he care at the moment.

He looked back at Slater. "What the hell happened?"

"We don't know yet. We'll have to check it out when things cool off."

One of the men called to Slater, and he headed back toward the office. Jared looked at the torched structure again and felt a shudder pass through him. If Annie had been in there...

He pulled her into his arms and held her, burying his face in her hair and breathing in the sweet smell of the silky strands. He wanted to pull her inside him, keep her where nothing could touch her, where nothing could harm her. He didn't give a damn about the office or anything else. Only her.

He took hold of her shoulders and held her away from him. "What the hell were you doing up on the rig, anyway?"

She raised one brow. "Well, it was certainly better than being in the office."

He frowned at her and she sighed. "Glenn asked me to help him with a reading on the drill pipe. Everyone else was busy, and with you gone, we were short."

"We were shut down. Finished. Why is that drill still running?"

"Jared." She wrapped her hands around his arms. Her eyes were bright as she looked up at him. "There's another fault. A second oil trap under our target zone. I just know it. I'm working with the seismics and logs to chart it now." She stopped suddenly and groaned. "At least, I *was* working on it."

Confused, he stared at her. "Arloco authorized an extension on drilling before you mapped the fault?"

"Not exactly. I authorized it."

Surprise joined the confusion in Jared's eyes. "Annie, you can't do that. It'll mean your job."

"It's there, Jared, I know it is. It's been staring at me the whole time." With a deep sigh, Annie turned toward the destroyed trailer. "Everything was in the office. The seismics, the logs. I can't do anything now."

"Jared!" Slater walked toward him with Glenn at his side. It took Jared a moment to realize that the young man was not a willing companion. Slater had hold of one of his arms and was virtually dragging him.

Jared stepped away from Annie. "What's going on?"

"I thought you might like to ask Glenn here that question. I just caught him trying to sneak out, not to mention the gas can and rags in his front seat."

"I was just moving my car," Glenn protested. His face was pale; sweat beaded his brow.

Glenn? Jared couldn't believe it. Glenn had always been the first one to offer help or work overtime if he was needed. He'd had a little problem with gambling, but still, he'd have been the last one Jared would have suspected of any wrongdoing.

Which also made him the most logical.

Glenn was shaking so badly Jared almost felt sorry for the kid. Almost, until he remembered that Annie could have been in that office. A sudden furious rage overtook him. He swung hard and clipped Glenn on the jaw, sending him sprawling in the dirt. "You could have killed Annie, damn you. I ought to string you up right here."

Glenn's eyes were round with fear as he picked himself up and touched his bleeding lip. "No! No. I would never try to kill anyone." He looked at Annie. "Especially Annie. I'd never hurt her."

"And what about the compressor?" Jared said fiercely, giving the terrified young man a shake. "And all the other mishaps around here. The lights blowing, the pipe twisting off. Even the so-called flu. They were all your doing, weren't they?"

Jared started toward Glenn again, but Annie stepped in his way and touched him on the arm. She faced the young man and looked him in the eyes. "Why, Glenn?" she asked quietly. "Why would you do this to Jared and the crew?"

Glenn's face twisted in agony. "I—I gambled. Owed a lot of money. Too much, to the wrong people. I was scared."

Jared's eyes narrowed. "Are you saying someone paid off your gambling debts so you'd do this?"

Glenn drew in a shaky breath and nodded.

"Who?" Jared's face was set in granite as he grabbed Glenn once again.

"I don't know," Glenn said quickly. "I swear. A man contacted me by phone. I never saw anyone. I was just supposed to cause some problems, but no one was supposed to get hurt." He hung his head. "I'm sorry, Jared."

"Sorry?" Jared dragged the young man closer. "You try to ruin me, you could have killed someone, and you're *sorry?*"

Jared shoved Glenn backward and looked at Slater. "Lock him up in the toolshed. We'll let the sheriff take care of him."

Myrna, who was making her way toward Annie and Jared, stepped aside and watched as Slater dragged his prisoner away. She pressed a hand to her chest and hurried over to Jared. "Jared, my God, what happened?"

"Someone barbecued my office," he said dryly. "You wouldn't happen to know anything about that, would you?"

"Me?" Her eyes widened. "Why would I know anything?"

"Funny, that's the same thing you said to Jake right after his barn burned down."

Myrna's face turned ashen. "Jared, how can you say that? You know I had nothing to do with that. It was that ranch hand Jake fired."

"You wanted Jake's land, and he had unexplained problems. Now you want mine, and I'm having problems. I'd say that's one hell of a coincidence."

Myrna looked desperately from Annie to Jared. "Of course I want the land. Your father left me with none of my own. But I had nothing to do with any of this. You have to believe that."

Jared didn't want to believe his stepmother was involved. No doubt she was guilty of being selfish and stupid, but he couldn't have her thrown in jail for that.

The truth would come out sooner or later, and if she was responsible, he'd deal with her then. Jared sighed heavily. It hardly seemed to matter anymore. He hadn't found oil, and he was going to lose the land, anyway. Whoever had gone to all this trouble had done it for nothing.

"Carlton looks tired, Myrna," Jared said. "I think you better take him home."

"Jared, we've got to—"

"I mean it," he said harshly. "I want you to go. Now."

She opened her mouth, but quickly shut it again as she saw the hard look on his face. She cast a pleading glance at Annie, then walked back to her car.

Jared turned away and headed for the rig.

"What are you doing?" Annie was at his heels.

"I'm shutting down."

"Jared, no! We can't stop. It's there, I know it's there."

He shook his head. "I can't let you do this. You'll be throwing your career away. You told me yourself you'd never jeopardize your job for personal reasons."

"I was wrong." She grabbed his arm and dug her boots into the ground, forcing him to stop and face her. "Sometimes a person has to go with what's in their gut and their heart. Every part of me is screaming to go for this, Jared. Please, we've got to try."

He saw the intensity of her eyes, heard the desperation in her voice. "Annie, we'll both be roasted alive for violating a work contract. We may never work in the business again."

"I'll take that chance. But please, don't stop."

He glanced up and noticed that all the men, including Slater, had gathered around. They stood rigid, waiting for instructions, their expressions anxious. They wanted to proceed, too, he realized, even though they now knew they were working without authorization.

He looked back at Annie. Her eyes pleaded with him.

"What the hell," he said. "I guess I'm not too old to learn a new trade."

Laughing, she threw her arms around him, then quickly let go as she realized everyone was staring.

"One hour," he said sternly. "Not one minute more. Not one foot more. No arguments."

She crossed her heart and nodded furiously.

He turned to the men and glared at them. "Well, what's everybody waiting for? Get to work." ◆

Forty-nine minutes, thirty seconds later, they were still drilling. Every member of the crew was extremely aware of each minute that passed and oil wasn't found, but no one more so than Annie.

The drilling had gone smoothly, but the soil samples being brought up the drill pipe showed nothing. She looked at her most recent sample, then stood, groaning softly as she straightened her bent back. She was ankle-deep in mud, bone-tired and starving.

She was also just about out of second chances.

For the rig, and for Jared.

He'd been worried about her when he'd driven up earlier and saw the office burst into flames. No, frantic, she realized, remembering the way he'd tried to fight off the men holding him down. Knowing what he'd gone through when he'd watched Jonathan die, she felt her chest ache. Even for those few seconds he'd thought he was watching her die, too.

She loved him. And as each minute ticked away, she was that much closer to leaving. It didn't matter to him that she loved him or that he loved her. He was too determined to deny himself happiness, and nothing she'd said had made a difference.

Damn that stubborn streak of his!

She had no idea what she was going to do when she got back to Dallas. She'd have no job, a broken heart and a life that was suddenly going to become very complicated.

She sighed wearily, then noticed Slater hurrying from the toolshed. The foreman waved to Jared, who was up on the platform tightening a coupling joint. She watched curiously as Jared climbed down and the men talked for a moment. She couldn't hear the words over the noise of the drill, but when Jared put his hands on his hips and a fierce scowl darkened his face, she had a pretty good idea what he was saying.

Jaw set tight, he walked over to her.

"What is it?" she asked.

"It's Glenn," he said. "Slater just went to check on him and he's gone. Kicked out a panel in the back of the shed and got away. There's no way of knowing how long. We've all been too busy to notice."

She shook her head slowly. "It doesn't matter, Jared. He won't come back here. Not now."

"He could have killed you," Jared said angrily.

"No. He made sure that office was empty. He never wanted to hurt anyone, I'm certain of it." She lifted her gaze and looked into Jared's eyes. "I never would have forgiven him if anything had happened to you, though."

He moved closer to her. "Annie, you look like you're ready to drop. Let's shut it down."

The temptation to lean her exhausted body against his was strong. She resisted, knowing that if she gave in while she was in such a highly emotional state, she might crumble altogether. She lifted her arm and showed him her watch. "We still have seven minutes and twenty seconds."

"Annie..."

She shook her head. "You know those runners who are so far behind they have no chance of winning, and even after the race is over they keep running so they can cross the finish line?" A dizzy spell came over her and she closed her eyes for a second. "That's how I feel, Jared. It doesn't matter if I finish first. I just have to finish. I have to cross that line and go the distance."

Jared looked down at Annie. He saw the fatigue in her face and in her slumped shoulders. But the determination shone brighter and stronger than ever in her soft hazel eyes, and he loved her more at that moment than he'd ever thought possible.

It doesn't matter if I finish first, she'd said. *I just have to go the distance.*

Her words hit him square in the gut with the impact of a freight train. He was an idiot! A first-class absolute idiot.

It didn't matter who was first. Whether or not she had loved Jonathan. What mattered was *now.* That she loved Jared Stone. And that he loved her. This—here and now—had nothing to do with Jonathan. This was about Annie and Jared.

She'd told him once that there was something to be lost, something more precious than what he might gain, if he didn't follow his heart. She'd given her heart to him completely, openly, and he'd been too blinded with pride and guilt to see it.

And now she was putting everything on the line—her job, maybe her entire career—not only for what she believed in, but for him. Because she loved *him*.

With a laugh, he wrapped his arms around her and pulled her down into the mud with him.

"Jared!" she gasped, caught completely off guard. "What are you doing?"

"There's no rule that says you have to run that race standing up, is there?"

Frowning, she pushed away from him. "Well, I didn't exactly see myself sitting in mud as I crossed the line."

He tipped back her hard hat and moved his face close to hers. "I know what you mean. I never exactly pictured myself proposing to the woman I love sitting in mud, either. Especially with half a dozen other men hanging around and a drill running overhead."

She blinked slowly. "What did you say?"

He gave her a crooked grin. "I said, I love you, and I want you to marry me."

"You want me . . . to marry you?" she said slowly.

After all he'd put her through, he couldn't blame her for sounding confused. Hell, he was still stunned himself. "When I left here earlier, I went to Jonathan's grave. I realized it was Jonathan I'd truly been mad at all this time, not myself."

"Mad at Jonathan?"

"For dying. For leaving me behind. For not listening to me and going up on the rig. Every irrational reason I could come up with. You tried to tell me all along, but I wouldn't

listen. I wanted to blame myself, but you were right—
Jonathan did have to make his own choices. Even if it
meant he died for them.''

Annie touched his cheek. Neither one of them cared that
her fingers were covered with mud. "I'm so sorry for what
you've had to go through.''

He shook his head. "We both went through a lot because we loved Jonathan. But like you said, we can't
change the past. What we can do is put it behind us and
start anew. You and me. The way Jonathan would have
wanted.''

He wanted desperately to drag her out of here, to hold
her close to him where he could do this right. But it
wouldn't wait. He'd waited too long already, and he didn't
want to waste one more minute.

"When I drove up and saw the trailer explode and I
thought you were inside, I knew in that instant that my life
was over.'' He tightened his grip and pulled her closer. "I
couldn't have gone on without you, Annie. Nothing would
have meant anything to me ever again.''

Tears shone in her eyes as she looked at him. "Oh,
Jared, I'm so sorry.''

"I was a fool, Annie. First I let my guilt blind me, then
my pride. But for the first time in years, I see clearly. And
what I see is you and me, a house, a yard and passel of
kids.''

She studied his face carefully. "What exactly *is* a passel?''

He thought about that. "A bunch.''

"Well,'' she said slowly, "do you think we could start
with just one?''

"Sure. One would be . . .'' He went still. His eyes widened and he drew back, his expression questioning. "Are
you, I mean, have you . . . ?''

She nodded.

The smile started slowly, then gained momentum and broke into a full grin. He let out a whoop, then pulled her to him and kissed her hard. They both fell back into the mud. The men began to whistle and hoot, but Jared just lifted one arm and waved them off.

When he finally let her back up, she could feel her face burn with embarrassment. She glanced down at her mud-covered body and laughed. "I took the test this morning," she said. "But this is hardly the setting I would have chosen to tell you you're going to be a father."

He placed a hand gently on her stomach, then looked at her with an expression so full of wonder she couldn't stop the tear that slipped from the corner of her eye.

"Are you sure?" he asked.

She nodded.

"Oh, Annie, I love you," he said, holding her gaze with his.

"And I love you, Jared Stone," she returned. "Even if you are covered with mud and you have black streaks all over your face."

It took a moment, but Jared went still at Annie's words.

Both Annie's and Jared's eyes widened as they stared at the mud surrounding them.

Black streaks? *Black streaks!*

Oil!

They'd struck oil!

Laughing, she threw her arms around his neck. He kissed her deeply, then pulled away. Desire flared in his eyes. She knew it was a look she'd never tire of seeing in that deep blue gaze.

A shadow fell over them, and they looked up to find Slater standing there. His dark gaze lit up as he noticed the black smeared on them. His grin was also as wide as the state the Texas. "Hey, you two noticed you're sitting in a pool of oil?"

"You have an uncanny grasp for the obvious," Jared said, and threw a handful of the black mud at his friend.

"Shoot, I know that." Slater winked at Annie and held out a hand to help to her up. "Looks like I'm going to have to find me another wife, too."

"Looks like." Jared stood and tucked Annie possessively into his side. "This one's taken."

Pandemonium broke loose then. Laughing and hollering, the crew gathered around, slapping each other on the back in their excitement. Annie gasped as one of the men pulled her from Jared's arms and hugged her. Every other crew member quickly followed suit, and she found herself in half a dozen pairs of arms before she came back to Jared.

She hadn't even time to catch her breath before he took her hand and dragged her up to the platform.

"What are you—"

He kissed her. A long deep kiss that left her trembling. When he pulled away and looked down at her, she saw the love in his eyes.

"This would have meant nothing without you. The rig, the oil, even this land." He made a wide sweep with his hand. "None of it would have mattered if you weren't here with me."

The raw emotion in Jared's voice brought tears to Annie's eyes. A breeze blew wisps of hair across her face, but she hardly noticed. "I am here, Jared. I always will be."

He crushed her tightly to him, whispering her name as he buried his lips in her hair. "I love you, Annie Bailey. More than you can possibly imagine."

He turned her in his arms and pulled her against his chest, holding her close as they stared out at the stark West Texas land called Stone Creek.

Smiling, she laid her head back against Jared's chest and felt the steady beat of his heart. She'd come home at last. This time to stay.

* * * * *

Look for TEXAS PRIDE, *Jessica's story,
the final book in Barbara McCauley's*
HEARTS OF STONE *trilogy.*

COMING NEXT MONTH

#943 THE WILDE BUNCH—Barbara Boswell

August's *Man of the Month,* rancher Mac Wilde, needed a woman to help raise his four kids. So he took Kara Kirby as his wife in name only....

#944 COWBOYS DON'T QUIT—Anne McAllister

Code of the West

Sexy cowboy Luke Tanner was trying to escape his past, and Jillian Crane was the only woman who could help him. Unfortunately, she also happened to be the woman he was running from....

#945 HEART OF THE HUNTER—BJ James

Men of the Black Watch

Fifteen years ago, Jeb Tanner had mysteriously disappeared from Nicole Callison's life. Now the irresistible man had somehow found her, but how could Nicole be sure his motives for returning were honorable?

#946 MAN OVERBOARD—Karen Leabo

Private investigator Harrison Powell knew beautiful Paige Stovall was hiding something. But it was too late—she had already pushed him overboard...with desire!

#947 THE RANCHER AND THE REDHEAD—Susannah Davis

The only way Sam Preston could keep custody of his baby cousin was to marry. So he hoodwinked Roni Daniels into becoming his wife!

#948 TEXAS TEMPTATION—Barbara McCauley

Hearts of Stone

Jared Stone was everything Annie Bailey had ever wanted in a man, but he was the one man she could *never* have. Would she risk the temptation of loving him when everything she cared about was at stake?

MILLION DOLLAR SWEEPSTAKES (III)

No purchase necessary. To enter, follow the directions published. Method of entry may vary. For eligibility, entries must be received no later than March 31, 1996. No liability is assumed for printing errors, lost, late or misdirected entries. Odds of winning are determined by the number of eligible entries distributed and received. Prizewinners will be determined no later than June 30, 1996.

Sweepstakes open to residents of the U.S. (except Puerto Rico), Canada, Europe and Taiwan who are 18 years of age or older. All applicable laws and regulations apply. Sweepstakes offer void wherever prohibited by law. Values of all prizes are in U.S. currency. This sweepstakes is presented by Torstar Corp., its subsidiaries and affiliates, in conjunction with book, merchandise and/or product offerings. For a copy of the Official Rules send a self-addressed, stamped envelope (WA residents need not affix return postage) to: MILLION DOLLAR SWEEPSTAKES (III) Rules, P.O. Box 4573, Blair, NE 68009, USA.

EXTRA BONUS PRIZE DRAWING

No purchase necessary. The Extra Bonus Prize will be awarded in a random drawing to be conducted no later than 5/30/96 from among all entries received. To qualify, entries must be received by 3/31/96 and comply with published directions. Drawing open to residents of the U.S. (except Puerto Rico), Canada, Europe and Taiwan who are 18 years of age or older. All applicable laws and regulations apply; offer void wherever prohibited by law. Odds of winning are dependent upon number of eligible entries received. Prize is valued in U.S. currency. The offer is presented by Torstar Corp., its subsidiaries and affiliates in conjunction with book, merchandise and/or product offering. For a copy of the Official Rules governing this sweepstakes, send a self-addressed, stamped envelope (WA residents need not affix return postage) to: Extra Bonus Prize Drawing Rules, P.O. Box 4590, Blair, NE 68009, USA.

SWP-S895

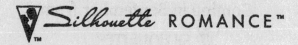

Silhouette ROMANCE™

Silhouette Romance presents the latest of Diana Palmer's
much-loved series

Long Tall Texans

COLTRAIN'S PROPOSAL
DIANA PALMER

Louise Blakely was about to leave town when Jebediah Coltrain made
a startling proposal—a fake engagement to save his reputation! But
soon Louise suspected that the handsome doctor had more on his mind
than his image. Could Jeb want Louise for life?

Coming in September from Silhouette Romance. Look for this
book in our "Make-Believe Marriage" promotion.

DPLTT

SOMETIMES BIG SURPRISES
COME IN SMALL PACKAGES!

BABY TALK
Julianna Morris

Cassie Cavannaugh wanted a baby, without the complications of an affair. But somehow she couldn't forget sexy Jake O'Connor, or the idea that he could father her child. Jake was handsome, headstrong, unpredictable…and nothing but trouble. But every time she got close to Jake, playing it smart seemed a losing battle.…

Coming in August 1995 from

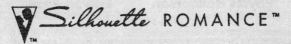

Silhouette

S P E C I A L ▼ E D I T I O N

™

It's our 1000th Special Edition and we're celebrating!

Join us these coming months for some wonderful stories in a special celebration of our 1000th book with some of your favorite authors!

Diana Palmer   **Nora Roberts**
Debbie Macomber   **Christine Flynn**
Phyllis Halldorson   **Lisa Jackson**

mini-series by:

Lindsay McKenna, Marie Ferrarella, Sherryl Woods, Gina Ferris Wilkins.

And many more books by special writers.

And as a special bonus, all Silhouette Special Edition titles published during Celebration 1000! Will have <u>**double**</u> Pages & Privileges proofs of purchase!

Silhouette Special Edition...heartwarming stories packed with emotion, just for you! You'll fall in love with our next 1000 special stories!

As a Privileged Woman, you'll be entitled to all these Free Benefits. And Free Gifts, too.

To thank you for buying our books, we've designed an exclusive FREE program called *PAGES & PRIVILEGES™*. You can enroll with just one Proof of Purchase, and get the kind of luxuries that, until now, you could only read about.

BIG HOTEL DISCOUNTS

A privileged woman stays in the finest hotels. And so can you—at up to 60% off! Imagine standing in a hotel check-in line and watching as the guest in front of you pays $150 for the same room that's only costing you $60. Your *Pages & Privileges* discounts are good at Sheraton, Marriott, Best Western, Hyatt and thousands of other fine hotels all over the U.S., Canada and Europe.

FREE DISCOUNT TRAVEL SERVICE

A privileged woman is always jetting to romantic places. When <u>you</u> fly, just make one phone call for the lowest published airfare at time of booking—<u>or double the difference back!</u> PLUS— you'll get a $25 voucher to use the first time you book a flight AND <u>5% cash back on every ticket you buy thereafter through the travel service!</u>

SD-PP4A

FREE GIFTS!

A privileged woman is always getting wonderful gifts.
Luxuriate in rich fragrances that will stir your senses (and his). This gift-boxed assortment of fine perfumes includes three popular scents, each in a beautiful designer bottle. <u>Truly Lace</u>...This luxurious fragrance unveils your sensuous side. <u>L'Effleur</u>...discover the romance of the Victorian era with this soft floral. <u>Muguet des bois</u>...a single note floral of singular beauty.

YOURS FREE!

$50 VALUE

FREE INSIDER TIPS LETTER

A privileged woman is always informed. And you'll be, too, with our free letter full of fascinating information and sneak previews of upcoming books.

MORE GREAT GIFTS & BENEFITS TO COME

A privileged woman always has a lot to look forward to. And so will you. You get all these wonderful FREE gifts and benefits now with only one purchase...and there are no additional purchases required. However, each additional retail purchase of Harlequin and Silhouette books brings you a step closer to even more great FREE benefits like half-price movie tickets... and even more FREE gifts.

L'Effleur...This basketful of romance lets you discover L'Effleur from head to toe, heart to home.

Truly Lace... A basket spun with the sensuous luxuries of Truly Lace, including Dusting Powder in a reusable satin and lace covered box.

Complete the Enrollment Form in the front of this book and mail it with this Proof of Purchase.

PROOF OF PURCHASE
Offer expires October 31, 1996

SD-PP4